The great and glorious masterpiece of man is to live to the point.

—*Michael de Montaigne*

I never claimed to have a license to kill, and I wouldn't want one. I didn't disqualify the mob from their day in court. They did. Only one law can touch them now, and that's my kind of justice —the law of the jungle. There are no judges here, no juries—there are only the living and the dead. So let's keep things to the point. Let's make them all dead.

—*Mack Bolan*, THE EXECUTIONER

The Executioner Series:

THE EXECUTIONER:
Caribbean Kill

by
Don Pendleton

PINNACLE BOOKS • LOS ANGELES

Dedication

For Agent J. L. Waymire of the Dade County Public Safety Department, Organized Crime Bureau . . . a cop who knows and cares. With respect and appreciation.

dp

Executioner Mack Bo-lan
Come for the kill in Caribe land,
Not here to play in the sun and sand,
Just come to kill all the gangster man.
                                        —*Calypso lyrics*

PROLOGUE

The beautiful scene below him was probably the most hazardous spot on earth for Mack Bolan—at this particular moment. But it was the one scene Bolan had been hoping to find, the mob's Caribbean hardsite, and the peril awaiting him there was merely another calculated risk in an impossible war which could end only with his death.

Bolan was willing to die—but not overly so.

The sleek little seaplane that had brought him here buzzed low over the rambling plantation house and rose again in a banking circle of the cozy, crescent-shaped inlet on Puerto Rico's southern shoreline. San Juan was less than fifty miles behind, at the far side of the island. The scenery below was magnificently framed around a small bay—more like a lagoon—with startlingly blue and glasslike water. It was probably a mile across at the widest point, with a man-made breakwater built across the opening to the sea and almost closing it.

The landward sides were edged with gleaming white sand—it looked polished, and was nearly blinding in the midday sun. Beyond the sand was lush tropical vegetation, in several shades of green, here and there wild bursts of orange and yellow, and vivid purples. To the north lay cultivated land, a large plantation on which seemed to be growing sugar cane and tobacco side-by-side in well-defined patches. Eastward from the bay was a high coastal plain and, away in the distance, a couple of small seaside villages. Backdropping it all were the high mountains of the interior, bluish and shimmering in haze.

Beautiful, sure. To many men, it would seem like paradise found.

Glass Bay would be no paradise for Mack Bolan.

Nor, from this moment on, for his enemies.

A weird set of circumstances had brought Bolan to this unlikely battleground of his war with the Mafia. The distance separating Las Vegas and Puerto Rico had to be expressed in something more than mere mileage; for most people, an entire world of ideas and purposes would be required to bridge that distance. Bolan, however, had made the leap while riding one idea and a single purpose.

The idea told it like it was: the mob is everywhere, into everything—squeezing, gouging, clawing, manipulating and controlling wherever bucks flowed freely —and, *like it was*, Puerto Rico and all the Caribbean playlands were identical peas in the same pod that housed Las Vegas.

The single purpose of Mack Bolan's life was to stop the Mafia wherever he found their leeching tentacles of influence—to jar their omnipotence, to confound their brilliance at organization, and to rid the earth of their oppressive weight. Others had failed in that purpose. The combined talents of law-enforcement agencies the world over had been failing for longer than Mack Bolan had been alive. Competitive syndicates and rival gangs had arisen to challenge the awesome power of *La Cosa Nostra,* only to be immediately snuffed out or absorbed by the invisible empire.

So what made a lone man, totally unsupported by anything other than his own wits and will, think that he could succeed where so many others had failed? Bolan himself did not consider such questions. In his own understanding, he was technically dead already—a man doomed by his own actions, by his own character. Victory meant living for one more day, and carrying his war to the enemy one more time. There could be no personal victory for Mack Bolan; this also he understood. His war with the Mafia had been declared on such an unpromising note, and each battle of that conflict was regarded as merely another step along his final mile of life.

It had all begun with five blasts of a Marlin .444, fired from an office building onto the streets of the eastern U.S. city of Pittsfield, in the ambush-execution of five local gangland figures.

Police authorities who investigated the slayings at first attributed the deaths to an underworld purge. It was not unusual for competitive criminal elements to engage in territorial disputes; the mass murder bore all the earmarks of a gang war.

But then the physical evidence began forming an entirely different picture. A local sports shop had been "burglarized" a few nights prior to the killings. A Marlin big-game rifle and a deluxe scope were missing, along with a supply of ammunition and a package of targets. A sum of money sufficient to cover the unorthodox purchase was left behind, and the shopkeeper had no complaints. He reported the incident to the police purely "for the record."

On the day following, the watchman at an inactive rock quarry just outside the city observed a tall young man in the act of test-firing and adjusting "a big game rifle." The man was apparently "sighting-in" the weapon and preparing trajectory graphs. The watchman saw no harm in these activities and did not report the matter until news of the slayings had been released.

The detective in charge of the homicide investigation recalled that a young soldier on emergency furlough from Vietnam had, some days earlier, been agitating for a closer police scrutiny of the deaths of his parents and teenage sister, whom the soldier had come home to bury. The official police blotter covering that earlier tragedy revealed an open and shut case of suicide-homicide, with the soldier's father as the culprit of the piece. The soldier had strongly protested this finding, insisting that underworld figures were at least indirectly responsible for his family's death.

Following a hunch, the Pittsfield police detective sent a query to the military police in Saigon. The reply, reproduced below, fully confirmed the detective's suspicions and laid to rest any ideas concerning a "gang war" in Pittsfield.

"Sgt. Mack Bolan—age 30—height 74 inches—weight 205 pounds, hair brown, eyes blue. Currently on emergency furlough, ARC verified, from Corps I area, destination your city. Subject known locally and respected throughout enemy strongholds as The Executioner. Penetration Team specialist, sniper. Holds sharpshooter rating, various personal weapons. Twice awarded Silver Star and holds many lesser decorations. Also decorated by South Vietnamese government for quote conspicuous valor unquote and quote humanitarian actions unquote. Career man, good conduct, second tour Vietnam. Officially

10

credited ninety-seven kills, execution missions behind enemy lines. Personally described by CO as quote formidable psychological warfare weapon unquote. Request full details any alleged civil infractions your city."

An army psychologist had these further words concerning Sgt. Bolan's specialty: "A good sniper has to be a man who can kill methodically, unemotionally, and *personally. Personally* because it's an entirely different ball game when you can see even the color of your victim's eyes through the magnification of a sniper-scope, when you can see the look of surprise and fear when he realizes he's been shot. Most any good soldier can be a successful sniper *once*—it's the second or third time around, when the memories of personal killing are etched into the conscience, that the 'soldiers' are separated from the 'executioners.' Killing in this manner is closely akin to murder in the conscience of many men. Of course, we do not want mad dogs in this program, either. What we want, quite simply, is a man who can distinguish between murder and duty, and who can realize that a duty killing is not an act of murder. A man who is also cool and calm when he himself is in jeopardy completes the picture of our sniper ideal."

Sergeant Bolan was that kind of man. That he maintained proper balance through two years and more of this bloody career is suggested by the other side of the Bolan ledger. Base Camp and Green Beret medics in Bolan's theatres of operation had quietly dubbed him "Sergeant Mercy"—an interesting contrast to the Executioner tag. It was said that the sarge seldom returned from a mission in enemy territory without an entourage of refugees who had become victims of enemy terrorist activities—usually the very old, the very young, the sick, the maimed.

It was this total portrait of Mack Bolan which so intrigued Lt. Alan Weatherbee of the Pittsfield homicide bureau and—though he had nothing to base a case upon—the detective knew that The Executioner had descended upon his town and that he was stalking another kind of enemy through the underworld paths of Pittsfield. Weatherbee was shedding no tears over the dead hoodlums—he would not have invested a nickel in a wreath for the mass funeral—but he also could not allow a self-appointed executioner to prowl the streets of his city. He pointed this out to Bolan, and suggested that the soldier return immediately to the more appropriate battle areas in Vietnam.

Bolan, however, had discovered something of his own, as witness this entry in his personal journal, dated the day following the initial slayings:

"Scratch five. Results positive. Identification confirmed by unofficial police report. *The Mafia*, for God's sake. So what? They can't be any more dangerous or any smarter than the Cong. Scratch five, and how many are left? A hundred? A thousand? Ten thousand? So—I've got another unwinnable war on my hands."

Yes, decidedly, Bolan had another war on his hands. He knew the Mafia, had grown up in neighborhoods dominated by the lordly *Dons*—he knew their power, their viciousness, and their patterns of intimidation which could never tolerate a successful retaliation from their victims. They would be after Bolan's head, and they would follow him all the way to Southeast Asia if necessary. If the police had been able to put the story together, Bolan knew with a certainty that the mob's own formidable intelligence network could not be more than a step or two behind.

He was a doomed man, and he knew it.

But, as he noted in his journal, "I'm dead anyway, I may as well make my death count for something. The cops can't do anything about the mob. The Mafia is a leech at this nation's throat and they know all the legal tricks and shady angles to keep themselves clear of the law. Besides, they're just too big. What they can't beat, they buy. If they can't buy it, they simply stamp it out. As they'll stamp me out one day very soon. But they are going to have to work for it. I won't just roll over and die for them. I'll die, sure, but while they're making it official I'm going to rattle their teeth and shake their house with everything I have."

For a "dying man," Bolan had a considerable amount of shake and rattle left in him. He hit the Pittsfield arm of the Mafia with a thunder and lightning blitz which indeed shook their house down and all but eliminated the Mafia presence in that city— for awhile.

Following that unexpected victory, Bolan faded away like the guerilla expert he was—believing himself to be ten-times doomed now, and determined only to stretch his "last bloody mile" to its highest toll of enemy lives. He resurfaced in Los Angeles a short while later, this time with a "death squad" of hastily recruited combat buddies from Vietnam —and the Bolan Wars began in earnest. He lost his valiant squad in the battles for Los Angeles, but he gained a new appreciation of the forces arrayed against him—and a deeper understanding of his own situation. And he began to believe that just possibly he *could* beat the mob at their own game.

From an old friend, an ex-army combat surgeon, Bolan received plastic surgery and a new face—not to retire behind, but to come out fighting in. He called the new face his "battle mask"—it gave him a definitely Sicilian appearance, and he used this new advantage with a vengeance in exploiting the enemy's greatest weakness: their own suspicion and mistrust of one another. He moved among them at will, sat with them at their councils, plotted with them his own demise—even romanced the *Capo's* daughter. And as he systematically set them up and knocked them down, the Executioner's understanding of this curious enemy deepened. He learned to think as they thought, to speak as they spoke—he became a master at deception and manipulation, and the death blows began to reverberate throughout the entire empire of syndicated evil.

Stung now to a total response, the farflung families of *La Cosa Nostra* assembled at Miami Beach for a summit meeting to discuss ways and means of responding to the Bolan threat. Bolan himself did not receive an invitation. He went anyway, and the summit meeting became a Mafia disaster on a scale never before experienced.

Bolan had many things going for him—nerves of steel, audacity, an utter contempt for death, moral outrage, the ability to discipline himself, military expertise—all of these, certainly, but perhaps the attribute which continued to spell success for this audacious warrior was an almost uncanny sense of timing. His hit-and-fade strategy had the Mafia bigwigs figuratively climbing the walls of their empire with frustration and desperation. Ordinary street soldiers throughout the country developed the nervous habit of continually looking over their shoulders, of going through doorways with extreme care and of sleeping in lighted rooms. The Mafia's businessmen doubled their retinue of bodyguards and sent their families on vacations out of the country. The face value of the murder contract let on Bolan pyramided as territorial chieftains added enticing bonuses to keep ambitious freelancers thick and alert in their areas.

Meanwhile "the bastard" blitzed on, surfacing here and there for a quick hit and an even quicker fade-out, and Bolan's "last bloody mile" became an ever-widening wipe-out trail which ranged across the ocean into France and England, then back to New York City for a pitched battle there and another quick fade.

Timing kept Bolan moving, kept him alive—but intelligence and planning and a finely tuned military poise kept him beating the mob at their own game.

Mack Bolan was more than a war machine, however. He was also a man—subject to all the dreams and desires of any mortal—and his soul was growing weary of its burden of continual warfare, unending violence and ever-flowing rivers of blood. He did not regard himself as a crusader or as an avenging angel—but simply as a man who was doing a job which could not be avoided. Many times he contemplated the comparative ease which death offered him. Frequently he railed against his "leper" status, self-imposed, which necessarily alienated him from all lasting human relationships. Occasionally he succumbed to a dark melancholy which drove him into deep introspections and philosophic searches.

Through all this inner writhing he remained Mack Bolan, the Executioner, one-man army *par excellence,* and through it all he developed a meaningful philosophy—or perhaps, simply, a deeper understanding of his own unique situation. In that understanding there was no possibility of a personal victory. If the mob did not eventually get him, then the police would. He was doomed, whether he surrendered or fought on—the only difference being that his doom could have some positive value for the world if he continued to fight the good fight. So, life for Mack Bolan had boiled itself down to the simplest of terms: kill to live, live to kill. Fight on, and go out like a warrior—or give up, and die like a caged rat. He did not regard the latter alternative as an option worthy of the smallest consideration. He would die as he had lived—to the point.

Though sought by virtually every police establishment in the nation, Bolan never fought cops. His war was with the Mafia and—whether the police accepted the idea or not—the cops were his allies, not his enemies. He also exercised great care to keep non-combatants out of his battle zones. There is no record of any innocent bystanders being caught in the crossfire of a Bolan campaign. It is known that frequently, in fact, he scrubbed missions and broke contact when it became apparent that bystanders would become involved, and several of these occasions were at great peril to himself.

It was at Chicago that Bolan finally came to grips with his own inner turmoil and accepted once and for all his place in the universe. "A man's character is his fate," said Heraclitus, the early Greek philosopher—and Bolan discovered at Chicago that this same truth applied to societies as a whole. He found

16

there a city chained by its own character, and he left it that way, though minus a few characters it would never miss, and continued along his wipe-out trail to Las Vegas, the city of chance and very nearly the city of Bolan's last chance.

The Mafia counter-war reached its greatest proportions ever at Vegas, and the national enforcers thought they had the Executioner sewed up for sure in this town where the comfortable end of the averages perennially rode with the house. Once again, however, the astute militarist uncannily read the offense and turned it to his own advantage—and he left Vegas with all the chips.

He also left with $250,000 of the mob's money, one of their helicopters, a pilot and an accountant, or "bagman." The helicopter represented but the first leg of a devious route to the Caribbean island of Puerto Rico—the money, "skim" from Vegas casino profits, was but the latest installment of a continuing cash movement onto the "Caribbean Carousel," a new scene of intense activity for the international syndicate. Thus Bolan's escape from Vegas was also his springboard to the next battleground. It seemed a virtual certainty that the survivors of the Vegas battle would recover from their stunning defeat early enough to read Bolan's play and arrange a reception for him at flight's end.

Bolan was a military realist, not a wishful thinker. He had known that the Vegas deception could last just so long, and was expecting the trap that awaited him at Puerto Rico. It was another calculated risk, little different than all the others. The important thing was that they had revealed their hardsite to him.

The next move was up to him.

A tropical paradise lay just beyond that airplane window.

But the Executioner had not come to America's backyard playground to gambol in the sun and sand.

He was living to the point, and he had come for the Caribbean Kill. Bolan was blitzing into paradise.

1: COLLISION COURSE

They circled low over the breakwater and dropped smoothly onto the glasslike surface of *Bahia de Vidria,* the pontoons taking a gentle bite and skimming along the water runway toward the beach. The pilot had cut back on the power and they were idling slowly in a soft glide for the seaplane dock, a hundred yards or so downrange, when the Beretta slid into Bolan's fist and muzzled into the guy's throat.

"End of game, Grimaldi," the Executioner announced coldly.

The pilot swallowed hard past the outside pressure of cool steel and muttered, "I don't get you, Mr. Vinton."

"Sure you do," Bolan told him. "When the engine dies, you die."

He divided his attention to lift the binoculars into a close scan of the shoreline. A signboard on the pier loomed into the vision-field:

GLASS BAY RESORT
PRIVATE

Beyond the pier lay neatly landscaped grounds and a rambling structure resembling an oversized

19

plantation house—a two-story job with verandas at top and bottom levels. Colorful cabanas lined the beach. People in bathing suits sprawled about here and there in the sand—all male-type people, Bolan wryly noted. Others strolled casually about the grounds or lounged at the railings of the verandas. Say, thirty people in plain sight. Two guys in white ducks and sneakers waited on the pier to dock the plane.

It all would seem perfectly innocuous, to the casual observer.

Mack Bolan was not observing casually.

Not a native Puerto Rican was in sight. No females, no relaxed frivolity, no fun or games anywhere in evidence. It was a set stage, sloppily done— no doubt, Bolan mused, the result of haste. They hadn't had time to get all the props out. Something inside a beach cabana was giving off telltale flashes as it reflected the strong rays of the midday tropical sun—a telescopic lens, maybe. The beach towels of the "bathers" revealed oblong lumps of just about the proper size and shape to suggest concealed rifles or shotguns.

As the plane steadily closed the distance, clumps of men on the lower verenda of the house began drifting down the steps and disappearing into the vegetation.

Yeah, Glass Bay was the hardsite. And it was primed and waiting for a gate-crasher in masquerade.

It was, of course, time for the official unmasking. Bolan had known in his bones, for several hours now, that his little game was over. And now the time had come to pay the fare for that wild-ass exit from Vegas.

By the numbers, now, very carefully. A single

20

moment would decide life or death for Mack Bolan—a very precise moment in psychological time.

The pilot had been with Bolan through three exchanges of aircraft. He was a versatile flyer, but hardcore Mafia all the same, and he knew all the tricks of illegal evasion. Here was one situation that could not be evaded, however, and the knowledge of that truth was pasted all over the guy's face. He nervously cleared his throat and said, "Look, Bolan, it's all in a day's work, eh? Nothing personal. I just follow orders."

Bolan said, "Yeah."

"I didn't know it was you until the switch at Nassau. And I still didn't know for sure, I mean nobody told me. They just said Glass Bay instead of San Juan. That was the tipoff, I mean I knew something was up. And I put it together myself."

"Sure."

The guy was reaching for life. "You got to believe me, I wasn't in on the setup."

"I believe you," Bolan muttered.

A strangled sound from the rear announced that the bagman was not quite ready to die, either. He was cowering against his bags of bucks and trembling as he croaked, "Me, too, Mr. Bolan. Honest to God I didn't know until just now."

"Okay, get out," Bolan growned.

"Right here?" the accountant warbled hopefully.

Bolan nodded. The pier was less than fifty yards ahead now. "Not the money, just you." To the pilot, he commanded, "Pre-set those controls for a quick lift-off. Then you follow Lemke."

"Too late," Grimaldi replied, sighing. "Can you fly this crate?"

"Watch me," Bolan told him.

"You'll never make it out of here now. They'll blow this thing out of the water before you can get it turned around. You waited too long, Bolan."

"Just set it up," the Executioner commanded.

Lemke pushed the hatch open and gazed apprehensively at the water slipping gently by just below, then he jumped and disappeared from view. The two men on the pier reacted immediately, and a sudden film of perspiration appeared on the pilot's brow.

"Okay she's set!" he yelled, and pushed himself clear of the seat.

The people on shore were beginning to look alive. A man on the pier cupped his hands and shouted something toward the house. A clump of men wearing bathing suits and openly displaying weapons broke into a run for the seaplane dock.

Girmaldi threw himself through the hatch and Bolan swung around behind him to punch a pair of Parabellums into the two agitated figures on the pier. They went over backwards, their own weapons firing reflexively and wildly, and Bolan made a lunge for the throttle.

That precise moment had arrived.

He gave the little craft full throttle, swung the nose around to the desired course and locked the controls in that position, then he moved swiftly to the blind-side hatch as the seaplane hunched into the sudden acceleration.

He had no intention of trying to fly that water bird out of there. The intention was to make the opposing troops *think* that he was.

A startled moment of confusion was all he'd been bidding for. And he got it, sliding into the calm

Caribbean depths just as the reaction-fire came crashing into the speeding craft.

Bolan remained shallow and concentrated on achieving maximum underwater distance. By the time he surfaced, the pilotless plane had reached flightspeed and was just beginning a rather ragged lift-off. It broke land with only inches of clearance between pontoons and beach, then rose swiftly in a steady pull for treetop level, winging through a sustained and withering fire that was reaching out from every spot about that lagoon.

He had miscalculated the guns at Glass Bay. For each obvious one noted during that hasty landing recon, three and maybe four were now unloading in a massive and determined effort to abort the "getaway."

The trajectory of that speeding airborne missile must have suddenly become obvious to all who watched; the gunfire ceased as abruptly as it had begun and Bolan could see energetic bodies hastily disembarking from the second-story veranda. All along the beach, men were erupting from places of concealment and sprinting toward the house.

Hell was winging into paradise, and everybody there seemed to know it.

The men who had raced onto the pier were now stampeding back toward land, and the grounds surrounding the big house had come alive with frantic figures lunging about in diffuse patterns of escape.

The plane itself seemed poised motionless in the air, like a football in a stop-action forward-pass replay on the Game of the Week, with the plantation house representing the only eligible receiver downfield, and with the chagrined defenders hoping to God that the pass was going wild but knowing in their sinking hearts that it was directly on target.

And then the plane hit, slicing in just above the second-story porch and punching on through into the house with a shattering roar and exploding flames. Bolan saw airborne bodies, one of them flaming like a chunk of flying shish kebab, and a shrieking hubbub of panicky voices was wafting toward him across the still waters.

He watched just long enough to assess the probable results of the hit, then he sank once again beneath the smooth surface of *Bahia de Vidria* and continued his quiet approach to the beach.

His departure from the plane had apparently gone unnoticed. He had seen a motor launch speeding to the other swimmers, Lemke and Grimaldi; chances were excellent that not even they had been aware of Bolan's exit. So far, then, so good. If he could make a landfall with the same good fortune, then maybe he would be able to climb aboard that Caribbean Carousel and give it one mad ride.

He had not continued into that trap at Glass Bay for the sheer thrill of living dangerously. Bolan was living to the point. He had arrived at the scene of the kill.

For Quick Tony Lavagni, the flame-leapt scene at Glass Bay was anything but comforting. It was too much like re-entering an old and familiar nightmare, that's what it was like, and Quick Tony had that sick feeling at the pit of his gut.

Not that Lavagni was worried about the damned joint. Vince Triesta was the head man at Glass Bay. Let Vince worry about the damned real estate. Tony had, in fact, already set Vince straight about that matter.

"Bullshit," he'd calmly told him. "My boys ain't playing firemen. We didn't come all the way down here to pick up your broken pieces. Put out your own goddam fires."

And Vince had gone off raving and waving his arms around. Some guys never changed. Bullshit. Tony Lavagni had come for Bolan's head. That was all. And until that churning feeling left his gut, he wasn't about to take away his boys' guns and give 'em fire hoses.

Guys were laying around, burned and blasted; some dead, some almost. None of Tony's boys, though. So these boys down here at Glass Bay had been living it soft. Tony felt sorry for them, sure, the ones that got in the way. In the meanwhile, Quick Tony's guts did not feel right about Mack Bolan. And until they did. . . .

He snared his chief gunner, Charlie Dragone, as the big triggerman ambled past. "Where the hell you going, Charlie?" he asked him.

"To piss on Bolan's ashes," the crewchief replied, grinning.

"I ain't seen no ashes yet," Lavagni reported.

The grin left the big guy's face. He clasped his arms over his chest and watched two of the Glass Bay homeguard as they struggled up from the pier with a fire hose, then he turned back to his boss to ask, "No?"

"No is right."

Dragone's eyes traveled the white sand beach behind him for a moment, then the gaze rested briefly on the scene of confusion at the burning house. "You think maybe he wasn't in that plane?" he asked woodenly.

"My gut thinks maybe that," Lavagni told him.

"Who was it, then?"

"We'll find out in a minute. Here comes Grimaldi."

A group of men were rapidly approaching from the pier, two of them fully clothed and soaking wet. Jack Grimaldi, the pilot, recognized Lavagni immediately and threw him a tired salute. "Hell, I'm sorry, Mr. Lavagni," he called out, sending the apology ahead of the confrontation.

"You should be," Quick Tony replied calmly. Then he grinned and added, "Or I guess not. You're a lucky shit, buddy."

"Don't I know it," the pilot replied. He and Lemke had pulled to a halt and were standing rather disconsolately in the presence of the *Caporegime*. The other men had gone on to help with the disaster operations.

Dragone's eyes flashed to the house as he said, "How about it, Grimaldi. Is that Bolan or isn't it?"

The pilot was studying the crewchief's face, trying to place it in his memory. His gaze slid on to Lavagni as he responded to the question. "It sure wasn't sweet old Aunt Martha," he growled.

"It was him, all right," Lemke put in excitedly. "Cold as ice. Death eyes. I'll tell you, I've never seen—"

Lavagni's heavy tones overrode the testament to Bolan's deadliness. "I suppose you lost your shipment," he said, eyeing the accountant with displeasure.

The guy's eyes fell and he replied, "He made me leave it on the plane."

Lavagni gave Charlie Dragone a deadpan stare

and told him, "So go piss on the ashes of a quarter million bucks, Charlie."

The triggerman sighed and scuffed his feet about in the sand. "Did we get the guy or didn't we?" he quietly asked.

Lavagni was staring at the pilot.

Grimaldi said, "What?"

Lavagni said, "You heard the question."

"Tony has a gut feeling," Dragone explained. "He thinks maybe the plane flew itself into that house."

The comment was given as very light sarcasm. Grimaldi, however, replied in cold seriousness. "It could have," he said.

"Shit, I knew it," Quick Tony said calmly.

"He had a gun at my throat. Told me to set the controls for take-off." The pilot shrugged. "Anything to make the gentleman happy. I knew he'd never get it off. I mean, I knew it would be a suicidal attempt. All I wanted was to hell out of there. But you're right, Mr. Lavagni. He could have pulled a fast one. I mean, all he had to do was shove in the throttle and jump, that baby would have lifted out of there with or without him."

Dragone snapped, "Goddammit you should've thought about that!"

"Fuck you," the pilot snapped back, "and don't tell me what to think with a gun barrel jamming my throat!"

"You guys shut up," Lavagni softly commanded. He walked to the water's edge and sighted out across the bay as he sifted through the wild array of thoughts which were chugging across his mind.

If Bolan had in fact been in that plane when it crashed, there would be one hell of a time trying to prove it—even if they should find an extra body to account for. Charlie had been certainly right about one thing, for damn sure—there would be nothing left but ashes, and ashes sometimes could be pretty damn tough to identify.

But now, take Tony's tumbling gut. And Grimaldi had given support to what the gut seemed to already know. Mack the Bastard had not come to Glass Bay just to roast hisself in a plane crash. Not that guy, not that hard case goddamn guy.

Yeh. Quick Tony had tangled with Mack the Bastard already before. And only by a medical miracle and plenty of trans-Atlantic political clout was Tony standing there right now remembering it.

Sure. There was only one way to play it. Since he could not *prove* that Mack Bolan had crashed with that plane, he would have to assume that he had not.

Lavagni tried to ignore a little chill that was quivering at his spine. He rejoined the others, who were standing locked in a stiff silence, and he quietly announced, "Bolan swam for it. So let's go find him."

Dragone sighed, cast a melancholy eye on the burning house, and asked, "Where do we start?"

"We start right where he wants us," Lavagni replied heavily. "The guy's a jungle fighter, Charlie. That's where he'll go. I want Paul—and Duke . . . get Joe, too. And they better have those maps in their pockets."

"Plug crews," Dragone decided.

"Yeh. And get those boat crews over here, they get a piece of this too."

"Can I go now?" Grimaldi asked quickly. "I need a drink."

Lavagni ignored the pilot's request. "Jack, you'll know who to contact, I want a couple of whirly

28

birds out here. I wish I'd kept a couple here, now. Dammit, why the hell didn't I think of that?"

Dragone was walking away. The *Caporegime* called after him, "Don't forget the walky-talkies." To Grimaldi, he snapped, "Well, move it, move it!"

"Yessir," the pilot said, and hurried off.

Lemke's eyes flashed uncertainly between Lavagni and the retreating figure of the pilot.

"Go help fight the fire!" Lavagni barked.

The accountant fled, leaving Quick Tony Lavagni, the terror of the Atlantic Seaboard, to stand a lone vigil on the waters of Glass Bay.

Yeh. What a hell of a note. Here was Quick Tony, again, with a goddam contract on Mack the Blitzing Bastard. Mack the Jungle Cat. And in his own element now.

A tumbling gut just couldn't be wrong. Quick Tony was on a collision course with his own fate. Yeh. What a hell of a note.

2: THE CROWN

Bolan sat casually in the top of a coconut palm at the western rim of the bay and field-stripped his Beretta, cleaning away the corrosive salt water he'd picked up during that long swim to shore. He reassembled the finely-tuned weapon and gave the same careful attention to the spare clips of ammo, finishing off with a close inspection of the muzzle silencer—then, satisfied that the Beretta Belle would serve upon demand, he allowed his mind to ponder the present predicament.

He was in an unfamiliar land, and with only the most general sort of geographic orientation. He knew that Puerto Rico was bounded on the north by the Atlantic, and on the other side by the Caribbean. It was the outer-most island of the West Indies. Hispaniola, the island shared by both Haiti and the Dominican Republic, lay to the west—also Jamaica and Cuba. The Bahamas were due north, Venezuela was south. To the east were the Virgin Islands.

All this he had quickly assimilated from a wall map at the private airport at Nassau, while the seaplane was being readied for this last leg of travel. For whatever it was worth, he at least knew approximately where he was located with respect to the rest of the world—and with respect to the new super operation which the mob was calling *The Caribbean Carousel.* It was small comfort at the moment.

Realistically, here was the situation: he had two full eight-round clips of ammo, plus six rounds in the service clip. He was literally up a tree, soaked to the skin with sticky salt water. He was hungry, and he was just about physically exhausted.

Less than a quarter-mile away, an army of some fifty to seventy-five guns was methodically sweeping the periphery of the bay in a determined hunt for his person.

He would very probably die in this jungle. And a grinning *Mafioso* would drop his head into a paper sack and deliver it to the grinning old men back home.

That was the situation.

Except that he was not dead yet.

Okay, he was alive and breathing. And it had not gone all that badly. He had broken out of the trap at Vegas and crashed the heart of the Caribbean operation all in one motion. And he was not dead yet.

Bolan raised his head and sighted along the beach toward the flaming house, trying to orient himself with respect to the birdseye view he had gained while in the plane. He was west of the house, about a thousand yards. Behind him, then, through maybe a half-mile of dense jungle, should lie the plantation he'd spotted from the air. The seaside villages lay in the opposite direction, with all of Glass Bay and its legion blocking the only practicable route of access.

Four motor launches were making a cross-grid search of the bay itself, another was just then disembarking a head party on the southwest tip of beach. These, about a dozen, would be working their way back toward Bolan's position. The main body of gunners were sweeping down from the house area. A pincers movement. With the jungle at his back and the open bay in front. And they were closing fast.

Bolan smiled grimly to himself and wondered who was commanding the Glass Bay forces. Whoever, the guy knew his business. And he had not been long fooled by the diversionary play with the seaplane.

The Executioner was going to have one hell of an interesting survival problem on his hands.

What could a dead man lose?

Bolan slid silently to the ground and quickly divested himself of the soggy suit of clothing he'd worn from Vegas. The fancy threads would be a hard liability now. He stripped down to the skintight black outfit which had become a trademark of the Executioner's war on the Mafia, transferring necessary personal items from the pockets of the discarded suit. Bolan was not impressed by trademarks. His interest was combat-readiness, and he knew the importance of appropriate garb.

He *was not, by God, dead yet.*

In a survival problem, a seasoned warrior would take every possible advantage, anything and everything which could make that hairline of difference between life and death. And a seasoned *jungle* warrior would push that difference to the limit.

The enemy was pushing ever closer. Bolan could hear their excited comments to one another as they swept along the beach. Apparently someone had spotted the point where he'd left the water.

He bared his teeth in a humorless grin and quickly arranged the wet suit of clothing against the trunk of a young tree. Under jungle law, the best man always won. That meant the quickest, the quietest, and the deadliest—and there were no juries to sway or clouted judges to appeal to. Here it was simply Man the Beast, reduced to his most basic elements and the rage to survive.

Bolan had been there before. He knew the rules.

He attended to final details, then he faded into the thick jungle growth, and merged with it, and became a living part of it.

They were allies now, he and the jungle.

And the Caribbean kill was finally underway.

At the time of his first run-in with Mack Bolan, Quick Tony Lavagni had been a lieutenant in the Washington-based family of Arnesto "Arnie Farmer" Castiglione, and he had been coasting comfortably toward old age with a so-so position in the national hierarchy of organized crime. But Bolan had brought many changes—dramatic ones—into Tony Lavagni's comfortable life. First had been that disastrous headhunting expedition to France, and Tony damn-near died in France. He had actually been reported dead.

Next had come actual death, for Castiglione himself, in England. Bolan, sure—who else?

What had followed was Family history, and not very pleasant stuff either, with Arnie's heirs jockeying for position in the new family line-up.

Lavagni had never seriously regarded himself as a candidate for Arnie Farmer's vacant throne. A wishful thought or two, sure, any guy would think about a thing like that. But Quick Tony had been not quite so quick to reach for those heady reins of power. For one thing, he was convalescing from that close scrape with death in France. Also, there were a couple others clearly above him in the line of succession, very capable others whom Lavagni did not really wish to cross. He preferred to play it cool, and almost surely he would be moved into an underboss spot regardless of who eventually succeeded to Arnie's crown. Tony was content to leave the scrambling to Weeney Scarbo and Big Gus Riappi, the major contenders.

But then, before the *Commissione* had time to pick the successor, another round of attrition started. Weeney had been in New York, politicking with the big city bosses, when Bolan made his hit up there . . . and Weeney had got hisself caught in that horror out at the Long Island joint . . . not killed, no, but enough of his brains were removed so he'd probably never be up and walking around again— hell, Weeney would probably never even feed himself again.

That left only Big Gus, and Tony was next in rank below him.

Lavagni had been in Miami, fully recovered now from that mess in France but content to lie about in the Florida sun for awhile longer, when the call came down from the top.

"The Talifero brothers lost it at Vegas," was the message, which could mean they were dead or anything. "We've got Bolan made, though. He's calling himself Frankie Vinton, and right now he's on a run to the Caribbean in one of our planes. We want you to get up a party and meet him at Glass Bay."

"Okay, sure, I'll be glad to," Lavagni had replied without hesitation.

"We knew you would. Something else you should know, Tony. We haven't made up our minds yet about the new head of the Atlantic Seaboard Company. You make a good show at Glass Bay and ... well, what else do we have to say, Tony?"

The thinly veiled promise had struck Lavagni momentarily dumb. When his voice returned he simply replied, "Yessir, I understand. How much time do I have to get there?"

"We're slowing him all we can without actually showing our hand. But you have, at the very most, six hours. You'll have to move fast."

"What if I don't beat him there?" Tony had wanted to know.

"Then he'll get met by Vince Triesta."

"Oh, well, I guess I sure better move fast," he'd replied soberly.

"We're making all the arrangements for your transportation, Tony. Just get a party together and get in touch with Jake Schuman for the rest. You're jetting to San Juan direct, helicopters on into Glass Bay. Jake will handle your financing and all of your materials requirements. You know. Recruit as many hunters as you can round up, keeping in mind the time problem. They'll be paid in advance as they board the plane."

Freelancers. Quick Tony had again gotten stuck with a bunch of goddam freelance streetcorner rodmen. So okay, fuck it. He'd known that Charlie Dragone was in town, also probably two or three other experienced hands were around, enough to build a force on.

"I'll want an open ticket," he'd told the commissioner. "I want authority to tap any boy around here that I like. And I want it clearly understood with Vince Triesta who'll be running the show at Glass Bay."

"Don't worry, Tony, we're putting out the word. He's all yours, baby."

Yeah. All Tony's. As quick as that. And Quick Tony had left Miami less than two hours later, and with a pretty good force after all, considering the sudden notice plus the fact that he was a long way from home turf. And it was not until he had settled into the cushions of the chartered jetliner that the full implications of the thing crashed into his mind.

God, he could come out of this contract wearing the crown of the Lower Atlantic Seaboard, boss of all that moved and breathed between Jersey and Jacksonville. Arnie Farmer's crown was still floating around, awaiting a suitable head to descend upon. And Quick Tony Lavagni had suddenly decided that his very own head was both suitable and deserving. And why not? He had been a loyal and hard working family man for going onto a quarter of a century now. His only serious failure had been that business in France ... and, hell, Bolan had disgraced better triggermen than Tony Lavagni.

Maybe, he'd decided, this was the *Commissione's* reasoning: give Tony another shot at the bastard, let him redeem himself. Yeh. And surely the guy who could come up with Bolan's skull would be worthy of something extra special for his own head. Something like, say, the Lower Atlantic Seaboard. Yeh. And Quick Tony had begun to dream of empire.

So what the hell, the thing had started going sour right at the start. No time for the setup at Glass Bay, and Bolan's goddam grandstand play, the bastard. So what kind of a nut should believe that Bolan would be a pushover? The guy hadn't won anything yet ... the thing had only started, not ended ... and Quick Tony was now satisfied that he had found the place where his quarry had come ashore.

He was kneeling in the finely packed sand near the waterline and running a visual triangulation between the house, which was about a half a mile downshore, and the encroachment of jungle flora, less than twenty feet away. The shoreline jogged slightly at that point, creating a shallow indentation which would be invisible from the house.

Sure, it all fit. "This is where, all right," Lavagni announced to chief gunner Charlie Dragone. He lifted an arm and sighted across the bay. "Yeah, and it was a hell of a long swim, nearly a mile I'd say. He could've cut that in half, but he was looking for cover, not comfort. And looka here. . . ." The Mafia chieftain was running the palm of his hand along the sand. "Still wet right here. We can't be more than a few minutes behind him. I bet that goddam guy swum underwater the whole way. Now . . . that can only mean. . . ."

The voice trailed away and Lavagni stared speculatively across the small width of beach.

Dragone rose nervously to his feet, standing in a half-crouch with both hands on his hips and gazed back toward the house. Smoke was still pouring out back there. Now and then a tongue of flame would lick clear of the smoke, a reminder that all was not over down there, either.

"You figure maybe he's circling back to the joint?" the crewchief mused.

"Naw." Lavagni stood up and spat into the water. Somewhere he'd heard that it was supposed to bring good luck. "After a swim like that he's probably all worn out. Probably laying low, somewheres in that jungle there, just getting his breath. What'd Grimaldi have to say about his hardware?"

"He only saw one gun. Said it was an automatic with a silencer."

Lavagni snorted. "That Beretta, probably. That's his hotsy, but it ain't going to be hot enough this time."

Dragone looked worried. He said, "Well the longer we wait. . . ."

"Let 'im run awhile," Lavagni said casually. "Who's got the walky-talky?"

"Latigo."

"Awright. You tell Latigo to get those plugs in place. Just the way we laid it out. And tell him not to screw around with this guy, he's bad news all the way. Don't give 'im an inch, not a damn inch."

"Okay." Dragone took a step forward, then froze and whirled about as one of his gunners moved quickly onto the beach and hoarsely whispered, "Boss! We found something!"

Both men hurried across the sand to inspect a soggy package of cigarettes and a paper matchbook bearing the imprint of a Las Vegas casino. The gunner was explaining, "We found it in the bushes back here, just off the beach."

"Where's Tilly?" Dragone asked quickly.

"He's in there, looking for tracks."

Lavagni hissed, "Tracks hell! Get that guy outta there!" He took his crewchief by the arm and whispered, "Get Latigo moving. Then get all your boys down here and lined up. No more'n ten foot intervals. Put the center of your line right here. But we don't start the sweep until Latigo says the plugs are all in. You got that?"

"I got it," the crewchief acknowledged. As he

moved away, he added, "Don't worry, Tony. The guy doesn't have a prayer."

Lavagni, however, was taking no bets yet. He fidgeted for a moment, then stepped off in pursuit of the gun soldier who had found the evidence of Bolan's passage. He wondered, just for the hell of it, if Bolan had *meant* for that stuff to get found. For a guy who was usually so damn careful, it seemed like a dumb mistake. But, why would he *plant* the stuff?

The Mafia veteran paused for a quick scan of the bay, then he shook his head and went on. The guy wouldn't come ashore, plant a false trail, then shove right back off into the water again. Not after a mile swim, hell no.

Lavagni found himself stepping into sudden darkness—compared to the fierce brightness out there on that beach. The thick overhead foliage of the tropical forest blocked the direct thrust of the sun, allowing the penetration of only a scattering of weak rays at infrequent intervals, and creating a sort of twilight effect.

Small living things could be heard scampering about in the dense undergrowth. Here and there in the distance the disturbed squawking of a bird rose above the ceaseless din created by hordes of twittering, but invisible, insects.

Lavagni shivered and moved on deeper, his eyes seeking an adjustment to the sudden change of lighting. Then he spotted the hired gunner.

The guy was frozen in an oddly off-balance stance, and he was staring at a man who seemed to be leaning lazily against a tree trunk.

The *Caporegime* fiercely whispered, "Come on, you boys get it outta here! We don't want to—"

Tony's jungle vision was improving, and the look

on the gunner's face cut him short. He moved closer, then lunged suddenly toward the leaning man in an involuntary reaction to what he saw there.

"What the hell ... ?" he grunted.

"It's Tilly," the gunner croaked.

Yes, Quick Tony could see clearly now, it was indeed Tilly. With eyes bugging and mouth thrown open in a silent cry. And he was not lounging against that tree. Hell no, he was tied to it, at the throat, a tough jungle vine almost buried in the soft flesh and wrapped tightly around the treetrunk and holding the dead gunner rooted to the spot where death had descended.

The disturbed condition of the jungle floor at Tilly's feet told the story in stark terms. In his mind's eye, Lavagni saw the entire thing re-enacted: a swiftly moving jungle shadow, striking without being seen even, or heard—and Tilly being whirled about and garroted to that tree with his throat clamped shut before a breath of air or an outcry could pass. Yes, Tony could see it all.

He could see something else, also. A wet suit of clothes was plastered to that tree, behind Tilly's dead body.

Lavagni reached past the corpse to finger the wet fabric.

"Let that be a lesson," he muttered, casting nervous glances into the trees surrounding them. "This guy is mean as hell. Now get outta here, and tell Charlie the guy is no doubt wearing his black suit now—or else he's running around nekkid, and I can't hardly see that."

The gunner had not moved a muscle, nor did he seem to have heard Lavagni's instructions.

41

"Well whatta you waiting for?" the boss hissed. "Get going, for Christ sakes!"

"I don't see Tilly's hardware," the other man replied dispiritedly.

"What was he packing?"

"A chopper."

Lavagni groaned and hurried his shaken freelancer out of there.

Yeh. The bastard had planted the goddam matches, all right. And he was armed with more than a lousy handgun now, too.

The thing was looking more sour by the minute. Yeh. And for Quick Tony Lavagni, the contract at Glass Bay was becoming more and more a crown of thorns.

Nobody who'd never gone against Bolan could really appreciate that.

Nobody.

3: HOME AND THE DEAD

A living shadow quietly watched as the two *Mafiosi* hurried from the presence of sudden death, and a mental mug-file review clicked to a decisive halt against the name of Quick Tony Lavagni.

Bolan knew, now, the identity of his chief opponent at Glass Bay, and the revelation gave no cause for a celebration. The crafty old Washington triggerman had built an impressive box for the Executioner on the French Riviera, and it had been as much luck as anything that had seen Bolan out of that trap. Lavagni was nobody's damn fool. He operated like a meat-grinder with radar control, quietly and efficiently bringing in all the corners of a battleground and wrapping them around a guy.

At least, though, Bolan had a fair idea of what to expect now, and he could respond accordingly.

Lavagni would be bringing his boats in to stand just offshore, appropriately spaced along the beach. He would send flankers around to cover the open ground at all sides of the small jungle area. Then he would mount a massive frontal movement, sieving in from the bay, and then ... well, it would be the meat-grinder routine once again.

In France there had been a friendly black face in the enemy camp and the soft hand of providence in

43

the person of a dazzling French movie actress to spell the difference for Bolan. Even in Vietnam there had always been the hope of making it back into home territory, or of making contact with a friendly force.

Where was home territory now? And where in all the world was a friendly force?

Bolan knew better than to even ask the question. "Home" was wherever he could find space to breathe. "Friendly forces" were the ones whom he could make dead.

So at least he knew where he stood. He was in the center of Lavagni's meat-grinder, somewhere between *home* and *the dead.* The Thompson submachine gun which he had appropriated from his latest "friend" would make little difference in any pitched battle with the forces at Glass Bay. There could be but one final result. Someone would walk away with Bolan's head in a sack.

The Executioner's combat-conditioned mind began quickly searching for a higher rationale to the situation. First, what was the enemy thinking?

They were thinking, probably, that Bolan had sniffed the trap at the last minute, and was intent only upon escape. They had him outnumbered, with the odds at about 100 to 1, and with one of their best field marshals leading the chase. And the field of play was very limited. They could afford to play the meat-grinder game, continually closing the sides of the box until they had him completely contained.

Secondly, what about Lavagni himself? Bolan knew enough about syndicate operations to be almost certain that Quick Tony was not the resident triggerman at Glass Bay. He had been hurried in from the states to arrange the reception and ... yes,

44

he would have brought his own force with him. Which meant a hasty recruiting job, probably among free-lance rodmen swept up from the street and jails of some American city.

Uh huh, so here was that larger rationale. The mob was expecting Bolan to spend his blood in an isolated jungle of America's back yard, against a ragtag army of mercenaries, while their prized little playground carousel continued merrily and unthreatened along its profitable course.

That, Bolan decided, was not the name of his game. He had come south to harass the syndicate and end their Caribbean operation if he could. If he had wanted to simply confront them and quickly spend his blood, he could have done so at any point along that escape route from Vegas.

The problem now, the immediate objective for Bolan, was to break out of that trap at Glass Bay. And to do so in such a way as to advance him toward the long range objective, the busting of the Caribbean Carousel—*the kill*.

Okay. Lavagni would be moving in his screen any moment now. It was time for a bit of psychological warfare ... something to jar the enemy, to slow them, to take away their iniative.

Bolan slung the Thompson across his chest and affixed the silencer to his Beretta Belle.

Right.

It was time to take the offensive.

Field Marshal Lavagni had his troops in place, and he was impatiently awaiting word that the plug crews were on station. A crude, hand-drawn map of the bay area lay on the sand in front of him, and this he was studying intently.

"How long d'you figure it'd take a guy on foot to cross this patch of jungle, Charlie?" he asked his chief gunner.

Dragone shrugged his shoulders. "Depend on the guy, I guess. It's probably slow going in there, though."

"Probably take me half a day," Lavagni admitted. "A guy who knew his way around, though. . . ."

"You figure he's making for the back side?"

"Yeh. That's what I'd do." The Mafia boss tapped the map with a thick finger. "I'd head straight for this sugar farm here. I'd buy or steal me some wheels, and I'd high-tail it for San Juan."

"That's what he's doing," Dragone agreed. "He needs to make some connections. I'd say San Juan, yeah." The crewchief scratched absently at his forehead. "One thing though, Tony. I doubt if this boy know where the hell he really is. I mean, without a map. . . ."

"He come in by plane, remember," Lavagni said, sighing. "Don't worry, this boy always knows where he's at. Did you tell Vince what I told you?"

"Yeh. I told him you want a complete rundown on all the civilians living in the area. He's sending a boy over, a native I guess, to talk to you. Soon as he can find him. Things are pretty tore up over there, Tony."

"They got things about under control?"

"Yeh, pretty much. But it's a mess. What the fire didn't get, the water did."

"Tell Latigo to send a couple of boys to the farm, this sugar farm here."

"Okay."

"*Good* boys."

"Sure, Tony."

46

"How about those whirly birds?"

"Taken care of. Grimaldi says it'll take about an hour."

"An hour from when?" Lavagni wanted to know.

"Well ... about fifty-five minutes from right now." Dragone heaved to his feet and motioned to a man in bathing trunks who was standing just downrange. "Bring that radio, Kelly," he growled.

The man hurried over with a small transistorized two-way radio and thrust it toward the chief gunner.

"Lavagni was saying, "Tell Latigo. . . ." and Dragone was reaching for the radio when suddenly it took flight, propelled with a screech from Kelly's hand by a sizzling lump of hot metal.

Another sizzler came in a heartbeat ahead of any possible reaction, this one squarely between the startled Kelly's eyes, and the man in the swimsuit toppled over and slid toward the water without a sound.

The other two found themselves lying shoulder to shoulder on the sand, their weapons up and searching for a target.

"Where'd it come from?" Lavagni puffed.

"It just came," the crewchief replied in a taut voice. "He got Kelly."

"Fuck Kelly, where's that sonuvabitch at!"

"I don't see a goddam thing, Tony. I didn't even hear nothing."

"Bastard! He's using his silencer."

Silencer or not, the line of gun soldiers flanking the two men had become aware of the drama at their center, and all were sprawled in the sand and anxiously watching for some sign of the enemy.

47

Dragone said, "I guess he ain't making for no sugar farm, Tony."

"He shot up the damn radio, didn't he."

"Yeh."

Lavagni was building toward a huge rage. "Dammit, we just can't lay here. Listen. Now listen close! Work your way along your side of the line, but dammit keep yourself down! Tell your boys we move on my signal. I'll take this side and clue everybody in on the action. When I get to the far end I'll fire two shots. That's the signal to *move it*. Tell each boy this, he's to stay in sight of the man next to him, I mean lookin' toward the center. That's important, so tell 'em. Dammit!"

Bolan's angle of vision onto the beach had given him a limited choice of targets. It had been like looking through a twenty-yard length of two-foot diameter pipeline and seeing clearly only those objects which happened to pass by the far end. Another foot or two to the right and he could as easily have taken out Lavagni himself, instead of settling for an anonymous soldier and a radio. Just the same, the message had been sent and received, and this had been the primary consideration.

He wanted those guys to get the taste of sand in their mouths and a fresh vision of death in their consciousness. And he'd wanted them to eat sand long enough to allow him a chance to advance to the next firing line.

That objective had been accomplished also, and now he was lying at the very edge of the forest, in a prone firing position and with good cover behind the rotting remains of a fallen tree. The terrain dropped away sharply just beyond that point, with the beach

48

sloping abruptly to meet the water. From his ground-level point of view, only the glassy surface of the bay lay directly ahead of him. Off to either flank, however, he had an excellent view of the activities underway on the beach itself.

To his right he saw Lavagni emerge from the blind spot, moving quickly in a low scamper along a line of rifle-toting gunners. The guys were flaked out there like a landing party in an amphibious assault, awaiting the signal to proceed inland. Then the other guy, obviously Lavagni's good right arm, appeared on the other flank in a similar movement.

Bolan precisely understood what they were doing.

He final-checked the Thompson and made a quick calculation of the firing angle which would be immediately available to him. He decided to set his limits at thirty degrees of horizon, then fed this into his observations of the enemy line.

They were spaced at ten or twelve feet. He would begin at dead center, and immediately sweep five degrees to either side. This should bring down the four or five closest threats.

His right flank was the most exposed, and the most vulnerable to an effective return-fire from the more distant points. So his second pattern would be sweeping out to fifteen degrees right, to at least minimize the retort from that angle. Then, if everything was on the numbers, he'd try to sweep some away from the left.

That was the battle plan. The entire fire mission should last no more than a few seconds. It had to be quick and brutal and over with before the enemy fully realized that it was happening. If properly executed, the play would mean, in actual numbers of those engaged, reducing the odds of the firefight to about 10 to 1 at the very worst. With a good automatic weapon, jungle cover, and the element of initiative in his favor, Bolan would ride those odds any time.

He watched Lavagni reach the far end of the line, saw the revolver lifting into the air, and heard the double report signalling the game to commence.

And then the line was up and running in a ragged advance across the white sands. Bolan's impression was of about twenty men to each flank, plus two rising up from the blind spot.

He spotted them three strides into the soft stuff, then the heavy chopper began its gutteral doomsday report. The two guys directly ahead were accorded the initial burst, each receiving a closely packed wreath of .45 caliber expanders in the chest. They went over backwards and out of view as the chopper swung on and the horrible sounds of automated death swept across the sands of paradise.

Bolan executed the fire mission to its planned parameters, no more and no less, and it was all over in a matter of seconds. Then he withdrew, back into the bosom of his home—the jungle, and left paradise to the company of the friendly dead.

Fire Mission number three was next on tap.

Lavagni and Dragone met at the center and re-formed their line, under the cover of trees—minus eight gunners who had not made it that far.

"What do you figure the guy thinks he's doing, Tony?" Dragone asked.

Lavagni was perspiring heavily from a combination of over-exertion in the tropical heat and strained emotions. "I don't know, Charlie," he replied disgustedly. "He's a hard case, that guy. If I

50

was him, I'd have been halfway out of this place by now."

"Maybe he didn't get away clean. From the plane, I mean. Maybe he ain't *able* to travel too well."

"It's something to think about," Lavagni admitted. "Anyway it don't matter. Look, I know what I'm doing, Charlie. Don't worry, the guy will run out of bullets before we run out of bodies."

"Don't let the boys hear you talking like that," Dragone cautioned in a hushed voice. "They're worried enough as it is."

Lavagni was about to make a heated comment to that when the chatter of the Thompson again erupted, this time from far along the line.

"Contact," Lavagni growled. "Let's go."

Before the two Mafia leaders could close on the new trouble spot, however, that third fire mission had been completed and the Executioner was moving swiftly through the jungle toward number four.

Bolan's battle plan was a basic guerilla maneuver. It was meant to draw the enemy line forward along a course of Bolan's choosing, to widen the spaces between the teeth of the grinder, and to slip through them.

This objective was neatly accomplished during the confused aftermath of the next brief firefight. Bolan stood quietly in the branches of a giant tree and watched the shaken enemy re-form their line beneath him and sweep on northward.

He noted that they had carefully collected the weapons of their fallen dead—and he smiled at this, accurately reading Lavagni's game of numbers. Quick Tony was willing to give the prey a few dead bodies, so long as he continued spending his precious ammo for them.

But that game was ending now.

Bolan was no longer concerned with the acquisition of friendly dead, and he had all the breathing space he'd wanted.

He gave the meat-grinder time to chew up a bit more jungle on the sweep northward, then he slipped to the ground and set off for the next objective.

It was time for a closer look at Glass Bay Resort.

4: GAME PLAN

The easiest and most direct route of retreat from Glass Bay would be through the jungle pocket, across the coastal plain, and into the mountains of the interior. From there, a guy on the run could probably commandeer a vehicle and make it into San Juan, a modern city of maybe half a million people. He could lay low for awhile in San Juan, then slip back to the states via ship or plane when the situation had cooled off.

There were two principal reasons, though, why Mack Bolan did not choose this avenue of escape.

First, the enemy would be expecting just such a move—and he did not wish to give them the added advantage of reading his game plan.

Secondly, Bolan did not choose to "lay low" in San Juan, nor did he have any intention of leaving the Caribbean until he'd completed his operations there.

The strategic route of retreat which he had selected lay directly across Glass Bay, past the enemy hardsite, and on beyond to one of the seaside villages. From there he would play it by ear and figure some way to strike at the mob's wheel of fortune.

The big problem of the moment was Glass Bay itself.

Bolan had moved cautiously to the eastern edge

of the forested area and he was taking a quiet reading of the situation there. He was about two hundred yards inland and looking southeasterly onto the grounds of the hardsite.

The fire had apparently been brought under control but smoke continued to rise from several stubbornly smouldering pockets. He counted twelve men moving tiredly about the damaged structure, a few still on fire hoses but most of them now engaged in salvage operations. Furnishings and other objects were strewn about the lawn. Angled to one side and out of the way was the line of Glass Bay dead, neatly lined up and wrapped in sheets.

Bolan grimaced and consulted his wristwatch. It had been a fast and chaotic forty minutes at Glass Bay.

His point of view was toward the rear of the house and across several hundred feet of open area. Four smaller structures were semi-circled behind the main building. None of them seemed to have suffered damage. Two were bungalows, one was a storehouse of some kind, the fourth appeared to be an office.

A VW sedan was parked between the bungalows. Behind these and set off at a right angle stood a long and narrow structure which provided carport parking for perhaps a dozen vehicles, with living quarters above. This would be the barracks, Bolan deduced, for lower echelon attendants of visiting big shots—the wheelmen, hardmen, etc. The place appeared deserted now, and there were no vehicles in the bays. So it followed that Lavagni's party had been airlifted in, not brought in by ground transport.

Continuing the visual inspection, Bolan noted an

asphalt road looping in from the east-rear section of the property. An arched gateway marked that eastern boundary. The blacktop road traversed the manicured grounds to the carports and ended there in a graveled circle. A dirt road led from there to Bolan's side of the compound, skirted the jungle for a hundred yards or so, then angled off toward the rear perimeter.

A jeet was presently occupying that dirt road, parked at the midpoint of the jungle stretch not a hundred feet from Bolan's position. Two men with poised Thompsons were standing behind it and intently watching the forest line.

Occasional distant gunfire was coming from the interior of the jungle area, in singles and in volleys, as the Lavagni meat-grinder chewed on northward. The survivors were probably thoroughly spooked now and firing at anything that moved or seemed to move. This suited Bolan fine. Another five minutes of that and they would probably be shooting at one another.

Meanwhile the pressure was being lifted from this corner of the battle zone. The two plug men at the jeep had noted the audible evidence that the sweep had progressed far beyond their position, and they were relaxing.

As Bolan watched, one of them lowered his weapon to light a cigarette. The other man said something, to which the first one laughed and moved around the front of the jeep to hand over the cigarette. Then he lit another for himself and the two stood chatting in low tones, their backs to Bolan as their attention remained focused on the distant sounds of "battle."

That jeep was Bolan's ticket out of Glass Bay, and he meant to have it. He was calculating the precise range from his position and applying this to the ballistics characteristics of the Beretta. The firing range would be approximately thirty yards. The Beretta had been worked-in for a twenty-five-yard point-blank range, meaning no rise or fall of trajectory across that distance, and the finely balanced weapon had delivered consistent two-inch groupings at such a range. The silencer, however, altered all that—and Bolan needed silence as much as he needed the jeep.

He was mentally calculating the corrections required when his attention was diverted by a commotion near the house. The Volkswagen had lurched away from the bungalow area only to be halted at the graveled circle opposite the carports.

The driver, to Bolan's surprise, was a woman. A big guy in a rumpled Palm Beach suit had pulled her out of the car and was dragging her back toward the bungalows.

The two men at the jeep had also swiveled about to watch the little drama. One of them chuckled and called out, "Atta boy, Vince"—though not loud enough to be heard across the intervening area.

Bolan pondered this development for a moment. Anything which was out of the ordinary deserved his attention, and to find a female around a hardsite at such a time was certainly unusual. Who was she? What was she doing there? Why was she being prevented from leaving?

He tried to shrug it off, deciding that the woman's presence could have little bearing on his own problem. As for *her* problem . . . well, maybe it was no more than a marital one. Maybe she was married to one of the Glass Bay wheels. Or she could be a girl friend, or the local whore-in-residence. At any rate, Bolan had enough of a problem already.

He pushed the woman from his mind and concentrated on his own problem in survival. One of his targets had raised a two-way radio to his head and was speaking into it.

New instructions?

It looked that way. Each of the men dropped his cigarette to the ground and stepped on it, then they swung around to opposite sides of the jeep and climbed aboard.

The Beretta was extended and ready to blast, the ballistics corrections being meticulously programmed through mind, eye and hand.

Bolan was waiting for the driver to stow his Thompson and start the jeep. The sound of the engine would be a further masking factor in the attack, and Bolan wanted everything going for him that he could get.

The finger squeezed home with the first crank of the engine, the Beretta recoiled with a soft cough, and the driver pitched forward across the steering wheel.

The other guy was turned in profile, caught in that micro-second of stunned realization before reaction sets in, when the Beretta Belle re-settled into the second alignment and another hi-impact missile sizzled along the doomsday course. It splattered in just above the mouth and sent the guy sprawling onto the ground, the Thompson still cradled in his arms.

The Executioner waited cautiously for some sign of a reaction from the hardsite. Receiving none, he stepped out of the vegetative cover and strolled unhurriedly to the jeep.

The engine was idling in neutral. Bolan went first to the man on the ground and dragged him around to the blind side. There was no recognizing that face. Most of it was missing. He was wearing a new sports shirt with a sale tag still attached and clean white denim slacks. Bolan removed the clothing and put it on over his skinsuit, and the fit was good enough for the moment.

Next he pulled the driver out and rolled him to the ground beside the other man. The Parabellum bone-crusher from the Beretta had penetrated at the base of the skull and angled up for an exit through a slightly enlarged eye socket. There was not much blood up front, and the departing trajectory of the bullet had cleared the jeep's windshield. Bolan tore the guy's shirt off and used it to sponge up the blood spatterings, then he retrieved the fallen Thompson from the roadway and added it to the growing arsenal in the rear seat.

The crew at the house were going on about their tiring chores as he wheeled the jeep into the soft run for the asphalt road. One of them paused to wipe the sweat from his brow as the jeep eased past.

"Trade you jobs, slick," he called over.

"Get laid," the Executioner called back, and went on into the traffic circle at the carports.

He was just about all the way home now, and already the air was smelling sweeter. Then his eye caught the abandoned VW, and a disturbing little tic began working at his deeper consciousness. He shrugged it away and continued around the circle, avoiding the VW, and pulled onto the blacktop.

Then he swore harshly to himself, swung on around the carports, and pulled to a halt between the bungalows.

58

Dammit, the woman could be in as large a mess as he was. He couldn't just. . . .

A man's angered tones were coming from the end bungalow. Bolan refueled the Beretta and returned her to the sideleather, then he left the jeep idling between the buildings and went on foot to the front.

A guy in wet, charcoal-smudged clothing stood on the porch. He gave Bolan a sour look and said, "Ay man."

The guy was no freelancer. He was a Mafia hardman and clearly in a nasty mood.

"Ay," Bolan growled back. "Vince in there?"

"He's busy," the guy said, moving into a tense confrontation at the doorway.

Bolan had no time for games, and he was feeling a bit nasty himself. He replied. "I see," as the Beretta leapt clear and pumped a quiet one up the guy's nose.

Bolan pushed the falling body into the house and stepped across it. The man in the rumpled Palm Beach was standing over a couch and lighting a cigar. He saw the dead bodyguard and the tall man with the Beretta and death itself, with one sweep of the eyes. The hand with the match froze and the guy took a dancing step backwards.

In a voice of clearest ice, Bolan told him, "I want the woman."

"Take her," the Glass Bay boss urged.

She looked Puerto Rican and very pretty, maybe twenty-five, simply dressed in a short skirt and cotton blouse. She was sprawled on the couch in a manner suggesting that she had been thrown or knocked there. The blouse was torn down the front, partially exposing an interesting chest, and she'd taken a couple of hard belts across the face.

The girl was crying and breathing hard, and mad as hell.

Bolan knew the guy, by mugshots and reputation only. It was Vince Triesta, a nickel and dime hood who'd made it big in drugs and girls in the Detroit area some years back. Before that he'd been involved in every rotten thing from shylocking to contract killing. He had, in fact, become endeared to the syndicate brass by murdering his ex-wife and her brother when they were preparing to testify before a Michigan crime commission. It had been nothing but roses for Triesta ever since ... until this very moment.

And certainly he realized that his time had come. "Take her!" he repeated shrilly. "I don't know her and I don't know you. You're Tony's problem, not mine. Take the broad and blow, and let's call it even."

"Not quite," Bolan told him, and he caressed the Beretta's nerve center once very lightly, and things were suddenly evened for Vince Triesta.

Bolan pulled the shaken girl to her feet and gently shoved her toward the door. "Let's go," he said. "*Vamos.*"

He preceded her to the porch and led the way to the jeep, and it was obvious that she was beginning to understand the situation as she scrambled onto the rear deck and curled herself into a little ball on the floorboards.

He told her, "That's the idea—*bueno*," and sent the jeep in a tight loop of the bungalow and onto the blacktop.

A guy lolling at the east gate picked up his shotgun and walked to the center of the road as the jeep approached.

Bolan slowed almost to a halt, then he stomped the accelerator and gunned ahead at the last moment. The guy was caught offguard in the path of the charging vehicle. The impact flung him onto the hood and carried him along for a few feet before spinning him off into the bushes at the side of the road.

Then they were free and clear and climbing a gentle rise onto the coastal road. The girl came out of her curl and climbed into the seat beside Bolan.

"Thank you," she said shakily.

"You speak English," Bolan observed. "Great."

She gave him a ragged smile as she replied, "I speak it once too often in the wrong place. It is my downfall. He would have killed me."

"Triesta, eh?"

"Yes, Triesta. He overhears me on telephone, in the little office. I think I am dead for sure. Except for you, I am."

Bolan was unwinding taut nerves and giving the woman a closer inspection. The eyes were wide-spaced, luminous, intelligent—almost contradicting the blatant sensuality of the rest of her.

"You've been staying at Glass Bay?" he asked.

"Yes, three months I am there."

"You could tell me things?"

She nodded and met his brooding gaze. "I could tell many things. If you are who I think."

Bolan returned his attention to the road and fought the jeep into a screaming turn as they topped the rise. Straightening out, he threw a quick glance along the backtrack. Glass Bay was laid out for his inspection. And it was a revealing one. A pickup truck and another jeep were tearing along the dirt road back there. Evidently the truth was out and the pursuit was on.

The girl had seen it also. She told him, in soft Spanish accents, "A man called Latigo coordinates their operations by radio. That is he in the pickup. Also they have sent to San Juan for helicopters."

Bolan reached into the rear seat and snared the radio he'd inherited with the jeep. He gave it to the woman and told her, "You be our ears."

She nodded assent and activated the radio, with no fumbling whatever.

The woman was becoming more of a puzzle. He bluntly asked her, "Okay, who are you and where do you fit?"

She countered with, "I would ask of you the same."

"Save it for later," he growled. "We're a long way from clear."

"And you are a long way from home, Mack Bolan," she replied.

"Right on," he muttered, not bothering to deny nor confirm the identification.

"You cannot remain on this road. There will be police roadblocks at Puerta Vista, the next village."

"How do you know that?" he asked, feeling already the answer in his gut.

She sighed. "Trust me. I owe you my life. I would not betray you. Go north at the next crossroads. I know a place of safety."

Bolan realized that there was little alternative but to play the game her way. He felt that wriggling finger of destiny tickling at his lifestrings once again, and he had learned to yield to its directions.

"Okay," he said tightly. "I guess I'm in your hands."

"And I am in yours."

"Let's set the game," Bolan said quietly. "I'm a wanted man. You're a cop. Now where do the two of us go from there?"

"I am also a woman," she reminded him in a small voice.

Bolan didn't need the reminder. From the top of that perfect head to those bare little feet, she was every inch a woman.

He showed her a reluctant smile and told her, "That was the first idea I got."

Her eyes flashed warmly to his and she said, "At the moment, I am *just* a woman."

Bolan could have told her that there was no such animal as just a woman. The female was the more complex and enigmatic in any species, and she wore many jungle hats. This one also wore a badge.

A small warm hand crept into his. He gently squeezed it and felt a responsive pressure.

"Okay," he said gruffly.

"Okay," she echoed, mimicking his gruff tone.

Then she laughed, a bit self-consciously, and Bolan laughed with her.

Into every jungle must creep an occasional ray of sunshine.

And they were approaching the crossroads. A crossroads in no-man's-land, somewhere on the border of hell and paradise.

Which way, Bolan wondered, led the road ahead?

5: THE PURSE

Tony Lavagni's report to the war council of bosses was an embarassing ordeal. His eyes were slightly glazed as he stared beyond the mouthpiece of the telephone and on to the scene just beyond the window of the office, as another sheet-draped corpse was being added to the lineup.

"The thing was sour from the start," Lavagni told his distant audience. "The guy had us set up right from the beginning, nobody can tell me different. And I mean all the way from Vegas. I believe he was counting on being brought here to Glass Bay all the time."

There was a long silence on the line, then a voice which Lavagni recognized as that of New York boss Augie Marinello came in with, "I guess you could be right, Tony. We now discover that the men from Washington have a certain black book that's giving them a lot of thrills. It turns out to be Heart of Gold Vito's last will and testament, mostly testament. We know also that Vito was closely involved with Mr. Blacksuit just before his—uh, untimely death. It figures that Vito's book was in our friend's hands before it went on to Washington."

"That's terrible," Quick Tony groaned.

"It's worse than that," another voice commented.

This one sounded like that little prick from the Bronx, the guy that took over Freddie Gambella's death-ridden organization. "Vito was too careful a bookkeeper. He had it down to dollars and dimes, destinations, names, the whole—"

Marinello's cautious tones cut in with, "Let's remember our problems with telephones, eh. The thing is, Tony, you're probably right. The guy is maybe on another bust. You know what that means."

"Yeah. Well I—"

"Of course we had thought of that possibility when we asked you to meet him there. And if you can't meet the guy at Glass Bay then tell me, Tony, where *can* you meet him?"

"It's not all that tight here," Lavagni explained in a muffled voice. "I had nearly a hundred boys on the reception committee. We had everything covered, and I mean all of it. It's just ... dammit, there's never nothing sure about this guy. It's almost like he's supernatural. You almost get the feeling sometimes that the guy reads minds or something."

"So what are you doing now to recover the situation?" Marinello asked.

"I got every car we had on the place out looking for him. I also got a couple of whirly birds that should be getting here in a few minutes. And I got in touch with our San Juan connections. They're sending committees out to cover all the roads coming in there from this part of the island. We got four big boats here. I sent them out. They'll check into everything that's floating, with the exception of the U.S. Navy. Soon as the whirlies get here, I'll send them on searching patterns from the air. Beyond all that, sir, I quite sincerely don't know exactly what else I can do."

"You can take some lessons in mind reading," said the little prick from the Bronx.

"What do you need from this end, Tony?" Marinello asked hastily, as though trying to soften the sarcastic comment from the youngest *Capo*.

Lavagno rode that wave of sympathy. He humbled himself to reply, "Whatever you think I could use, sir."

It didn't work. "Okay," the big boss told him. "I'm glad to see you're thinking straight, Tony. Pride goes before the fall, eh? So you won't think it's a slap in your face if we sent Gus Riappi down to lend a hand."

Quick Tony choked back his displeasure at the suggestion as he replied, "Course not, sir. All I want is to stop this guy. I don't care about nothing else right now. I've worked for Gus before, I can—"

"You won't be working *for* him, Tony. We're just splitting the territory. You keep on working that end. Follow wherever the trail leads."

"Right, I'll follow it to hell if I have to."

"That's the idea. Meanwhile Gus will be working some other angles."

Lavagni cleared a lump from his throat and said, "The—uh—the Vito book thing?"

"Right. We've cooled everything, naturally, and we'll be setting up a new chain. But we're also going to dummy the old one along. Just for our friend's benefit. We figure maybe he'll come right to us."

"He came right to us at Glass Bay," Lavagni commented darkly.

"Don't remind me," Marinello replied coldly. "I

don't have to tell you how disappointed I am, Tony."

"Yessir. Well, uh, we can't write this one off yet. And with me and Gus working towards each other, surely we'll . . . uh, Gus knows how I work so I guess he won't be getting in my way."

Marinello chuckled and said, "Well come to think of it, Tony, I guess this does develop into a horse race, doesn't it. Winner take all, eh?"

Lavagni understood perfectly. He replied, "Right, sir, I get you."

"Just get Mr. Blacksuit, Tony."

"You make book on that, sir."

The connection went dead and Lavagni slowly hung up. He turned to Charlie Dragone with a tired sigh and told him, "I don't blame them; they're terrible disappointed."

"What'd they say about Triesta?" Dragone wondered aloud.

"I didn't hear any tears splashing off the table." Lavagni sighed again. "They're sending down a replacement. They better replace the whole joint. I wonder how we managed to keep the telephone line."

"Did I hear you say something about Gus? Big Gus Riappi?"

"Yeh," Lavagni growled. "They're giving him a piece of the action." He got to his feet and walked out of the office, shielding his eyes against the bright sunlight and gazing into the skies.

Dragone followed him outside. "Just a piece?" he asked.

"Yeh. They've put us in a horse race. Winner take all."

"What's that mean, Tony?"

"It means that whichever one of us gets Bolan also gets to sit at Arnie Farmer's vacant desk, that's what it means."

"God, you mean. . .?"

"Yeh." Lavagni lit a cigar and watched the smoke drift skyward. "I think I hear those whirly birds. It's about damn time."

Dragone was looking at the potential *Capo* with new eyes. "You mean you'll be going clear to the top?"

"With Bolan's head in my sack, yeah." Lavagni took a hard pull at the cigar and sent his companion a sidewise glance as he exhaled the smoke. "How'd you like to change families, Charlie?"

The veteran triggerman took his time in replying. "I'd have to think about it," he said slowly. "I kinda like it where I'm at. But I ... well, I guess if there was something in it. . . ."

"Would you think there was something in standing at the right hand of a *Capo*, Charlie?"

"Listen Tony ... you know better than to ask. I mean, if you mean. . . ."

"That's exactly what I mean, Charlie. Listen. We got to put a sack on Bolan's head."

The exultant glow in the triggerman's eyes was already hardening to a calculated determination. "Where do we start?" he asked.

"Get on the radio and see if Latigo has anything yet. Then pass the word, there's a ten thou' bonus for the boy that comes up with Bolan's tracks, twenty-five-thou' for the one that brings in his head."

"That'll put some lead in their peters," Dragone agreed.

"I hope they get a hard that never goes down,"

Lavagni said. "I want them to *want* this boy, Charlie. The same way that you and I want him."

"Offer the contract purse, boss."

"Huh?"

"Give 'em something to *really* scramble for."

Quick Tony was weighing the idea. By the time the various territorial bonuses were tacked on, that contract was worth somewhere around a cool quarter-mil'. It was a hell of a lot of money. On a head-party expedition such as this, the pay-off ordinarily went to the contractor in charge, with the split going however he wished to make it.

"Well," he said musingly, "the man said winner takes all. That purse is peanuts compared to. . . . Okay. The boy that comes in with Bolan's head gets the purse, all of it, the whole thing. You pass that around, Charlie."

"You just bought yourself a crew of man-eating tigers," Dragone replied, grinning. He hurried away to spread the news, and Quick Tony resumed his scan of the skies.

He hoped that he was buying Bolan's head. At a quarter-mil, that would be the sharpest deal a guy could ever hope for. Yeh. It would be a horse race well worth the price of winning. Big Gus, of course, could be thinking the same way.

Lavagni fidgeted and watched the helicopters swoop in over Glass Bay. Yeh. It was going to be one hell of a horse race.

Steady monitoring of the enemy's radio signals had produced the temporarily comforting conclusion that the hounds of hell were off the track and ranging far east of the retreat route. And, for Bolan, the

70

end of a network of dusty trails was an isolated shack, several miles inland and well buried in the agricultural maze of the coastal plateau.

He pulled the jeep into a wooded area near the house and covered it with brush while the woman went on to clear the way for him with her friends. Before Bolan had completed the camouflage job, a slightly built youth of perhaps twenty-one or twenty-two emerged from the cabin and stood quietly watching him.

Bolan threw him a friendly wave and went on with his task. A moment later the Puerto Rican was standing beside him, a cautious smile on his face. "I will help, *señor*," he offered.

Bolan returned the smile and said, "Sure." He slung a Thompson across his chest and passed the other two to the youth. "You can take these inside."

The boy whistled softly under his breath and accepted the weapons.

"Call me Mack," Bolan told him.

The smile returned, stronger. "I am Juan Escadrillo."

"This your place, Juan?"

"*Si*, this place is mine."

"I won't be staying long," Bolan said. "Who else is here?"

"Rosalita, my wife."

"No kids?"

"Now, no. Soon, yes." He grinned. "One is in the belly."

Bolan turned away to mask the sudden displeasure he was feeling. This would be no good. A kid and his pregnant wife—Bolan had no wish to involve them in his troubles. So . . . perhaps a moment

71

of relaxation, a bite of food, and he would be on his way.

The woman reappeared in the yard, the radio slung from her shoulder. "Will you come inside?" she called.

"In a minute," Bolan replied. He told the boy, "Take the weapons in, Juan. I'll be along."

Escadrillo gave him a fleeting smile and set off for the house, a Thompson balanced jauntily across each shoulder.

Bolan then undertook a routine reconnaisance of the area, taking particular note of the terrain layout and orienting himself with the compass points. He was on relatively high ground and in a patchwork area of small truck-farms. He circled about to a hillside south of the house, and from there he could see the Caribbean, glisteningly blue in the afternoon haze. Off to the east were patches of wild growth and untended fields which were reverting to the jungle. To the north, at a somewhat higher elevation, was evidence of a strip-mining operation.

As he returned to the house, Bolan pondered the information given him by the woman who had brought him here. Her name was Evita Aguilar. She was twenty-six, single, and an agent of the Puerto Rican counterpart of the U.S. Justice Department, Organized Crime Division.

For three months she had been "cultivating" Vince Triesta and observing the visitors to Glass Bay. During that period, she had been Triesta's woman.

Bolan did not disrespect her for that.

In a war like this one, conventional morality was often the greater of two evils. *Right* was getting the

72

mob before it gobbled up everything in sight. *Wrong* was not doing so.

Bolan understood. It was his own philosophy. Hit them with every damn thing you have. And a woman had a unique advantage when it came to infiltrating the enemy. Why disrespect her for using her greatest weapon? Bolan did not.

Evita Aguilar was a gal with a cause. She had told Bolan, during that wild jeep ride, "This syndicate is hoping to take from our Operation Bootstrap. This is an economic development program, and it is badly needed in this land of the poor. I will not let these *Mafiosi* take the bread from my people's mouths. Sometimes we must fight the devil with the devil."

Exactly what Bolan himself was doing.

"Since Bootstrap," she'd added, "the per capita income has nearly doubled. This means a great flow of money, new money, at all levels of our economy. The syndicate would divert this flow to their own pockets."

"Yeah," he'd commented. "A five letter word beginning with M is both Money and Mafia."

"Or D," Evita said. "For *Dinero* and Devils."

Yeah, she was a gal with a cause. And Bolan was glad she was on his side, if only unofficially.

"We have known of you in San Juan since your very beginning," she'd told him. "Officially, of course, our position is that you are a criminal. We would apprehend you and extradite you to the mainland, if you should ever come to Puerto Rico. Unofficially, of course. . . ."

She'd left the rest of it unsaid, but Bolan knew what she'd meant. Many people in her department felt that they were in a life or death struggle with the Mafia octopus, and they would be happy to have all the help they could get. She had made it clear, though, that Bolan must not expose himself needlessly to the authorities.

"Not all of us have the flexibility to take unofficial positions," she explained.

It was the name of the game for Bolan. He understood.

He also understood Evita Aguilar. She was a social worker turned cop; a concerned citizen who had seen social justice crumbling under the pressures of organized cannibalism—and she'd decided to attack the problem at its source.

"This syndicate is corrupting district officials and looting the economy at all levels," she'd explained. "But it is the poor people who suffer the greatest loss. Is it not always so?"

Yes, Bolan knew, it was always so. The Mafia game was no more than the old European feudal system, dressed up for the twenty century and operating invisibly. In its gentlest form it was a method of "taxation without representation," an unconscionable gouging and exploitation of the economy of a people. It was the invisible hand forever in the pocket of the consumer. The corruptor of a nation's morals and of its government. Looter and rapist of industry and labor alike, temptress and panderer, and cheerleader to mass-man's baser appetites and needs.

In harsher variations it was contract murder, intimidation, white slavery, manipulation of competitive sports, narcotics, unrestrained political power, bigtime theft, black marketry—the whole wide range of criminal conspiracy.

Bolan had framed his reply to Evita in characteristic terseness, however. "A guy I met in Vegas," he'd told her, "wrapped up the whole rotten mess in just four words. Ants at a picnic. That's the mob. They don't build or produce, they just plunder. And wherever the picnic is, that's where you'll find them swarming. Where are the picnics in the Caribbean, Evita?"

She had raised her shoulders in a gentle shrug and replied, "Everywhere. Caribe land is the new swinging scene, and not merely for the idle rich. From the Bahamas throughout the West Indies and the Antilles, this is where the action is. The picnic, yes, the one *big* picnic."

"The Caribbean Carousel," he'd commented musingly.

"I have heard this term and wondered about it," the girl replied. "I am sometimes handicapped with the language, you see. Spanish is our official language but English is required teaching in all public schools. And in English, the carousel is a . . . a . . . !"

She was making a circular motion with her hands. Bolan grinned and helped her complete the idea. "Yeah, a circular horse race without a start or a finish—a merry-go-round."

"Ah yes. The British call it a round-a-bout. In the Italian, this word is *carosello*, originally meaning a tournament."

"Well, maybe that comes closer to the real meaning," Bolan had commented. "As the mob uses it, I mean. I believe you could help me get into that tournament, Evita."

"I will do what I can," she had promised him.

And now as Bolan returned to the shanty cabin in Puerto Rico's back country, he found himself wondering if any of it was really worthwhile, after all. Here was a lovely young woman, obviously well

75

educated and strongly principled, offering herself up body and soul as a sacrificial victim to the gods of human justice—and to what damned end?

Long after Evita Aguilar had been fully and finally desecrated, long after she had ceased to exist altogether—wouldn't the ants still be swarming at every human picnic?

Well . . . that was what life was all about, wasn't it? It was neither the picnics nor the ants that made humanity worthwhile. It was the struggle itself, the fight for balance—and the sacrifices that some humans were willing to make to maintain that balance.

Sure, Bolan understood.

It was the story of his own life.

Evita was waiting for him at the doorway.

She smiled and waved to him and called out, "The food is waiting. Come in and meet your friends."

Bolan understood that, also.

He took her arm and went inside to warm human companionship and a moment of relaxation.

In a little while the hell would begin again and the Caribbean *carosello* would resume at full gallop.

For now, it was enough to simply re-discover and remember what it was all about. The horse race without beginning or end could wait awhile.

For the moment, Mack Bolan was home . . . and remembering.

6: THE PARALLELS

The Escadrillo kids were obviously very much in love and caught up in the adventure of establishing home and family—as humble as the home and as tentative as the family might be. The girl appeared to be about six months pregnant. She was a pretty little thing with long black hair and glistening eyes—and beginning to move a bit clumsily with her extra burden. *Rosalita*, the little rose, was the perfect name for her, Bolan decided. She spoke very little English and at first seemed a bit awed with Bolan's presence in her home. He bridged their communications gap with an occasional complimentary phrase from his limited knowledge of her language, and they got a thing going with the eyes which transcended language barriers.

It was a simple meal, but the food was plentiful and tasty—and there were no social tensions in the Escadrillo household by meal's end.

The cabin was a single large room with a sleeping loft. It was spotlessly clean. The furnishings and decorations were minimal and inexpensive, but the end effect was surprisingly attractive and comfortable.

They had inside plumbing and electricity, a few modern gadgets in the kitchen area, a television set that didn't work and an impressive looking multi-band radio that did.

The bathroom was a mere closet with a toilet fixture. A small porcelain-enameled bathtub was plumbed to a corner of the open living area and shielded from public view only by a thin curtain on an overhead rod.

The fancy radio had been a gift from Evita. Juan was a short-wave addict. He kept a log of foreign broadcast stations and their schedules. He was also an informal student of languages and had spent many hours at that radio. Evita had provided him with a collection of language textbooks, which showed evidence of heavy use.

The kids had purchased the five-acre truckfarm via a government-subsidized loan program. Part of Operation Bootstrap, Bolan assumed. They also owned an ancient one-ton flatbed truck which Juan used to haul his produce to the marketplaces of San Juan. He did not plan to be a farmer forever, though. "One day," he told Bolan, "I will work as a linguist—an interpreter. Maybe I will work for the United Nations."

The young couple were aware of Bolan's situation. Evita had explained the problem at the outset; still, they had welcomed him as an honored guest and seemed to be planning on him remaining for an extended stay.

But Bolan was not so certain that they fully understood all the implications of his visit. As the women cleared the table, he caught Juan's eye and stepped outside to light a cigarette.

The youth followed him through the doorway and told him, "It is all right, *Señor* Bolan. You may smoke inside."

"I want to talk to you," Bolan explained. "One guy to another."

"*Si*. Talk."

"I'm leaving pretty quick. Don't misunderstand. I appreciate your hospitality. But I'm a walking plague, Juan. The hounds of hell are after me. Sooner or later they'll find me. I don't want them to find me here."

The boy fidgeted and stared at the ground. "I will help you," he stated quietly. "Show me how to shoot the big gun."

"No good," Bolan said. "There's more to making war than shooting a gun. When death is staring at you, or when blood starts flowing, you suddenly lose everything that's human. If you're not trained for that sort of thing, you're left with nothing but blind reaction. A trained soldier is programmed into certain instinctive actions. I can't program you, Juan, simply by showing you where the trigger is on a gun."

"I can be of help," the boy insisted.

"Sure you could, but not enough," Bolan told him. "If the headhunters find me here, blood will flow. And not just yours and mine." He jerked his head toward the cabin. "Their's too. So I've got to move on."

"I will help you to move on, then. Unless it is that you do not trust me."

"You know better than that." Bolan looked into the sky and tried to estimate the angle between the sun and the western horizon. "We're pretty close to the equator, aren't we," he murmured.

"*Si*, about 20 degrees north latitude." The boy smiled and somewhat shyly added, "I do not know

79

this until I study my radio propagation tables. It is a good thing to know, yes?"

Bolan sighed. "Yes, Juan, it's always a good idea to know where you are. And 20 degrees north also happens to be where South Vietnam is at. Isn't that a hell of a parallel." He grimaced and added, "Would you say we have about two hours of daylight left?"

"Yes, this is true."

Bolan was trying to weigh the thing in his mind, but Juan beat him to the decision. "You will stay at least until darkness comes," the Puerto Rican insisted. "And then I will guide you wherever you wish to go."

"That makes sense," Bolan agreed. His attention swiveled northward. "I saw an open pit mine or something a few miles onto the high ground. What are they mining?"

Juan shrugged his shoulders. "I think construction materials. Gravel, maybe. Maybe cement."

"They do any blasting?"

"Blasting? Oh, explosives. *Si*, sometimes."

"If you were going to charter a boat," Bolan asked, quickly changing the subject, "how much money would you figure you'd need?"

"What kind of a boat, *señor*?"

"Something capable of inter-island travel, a deep water job with a motor."

"As cheaply as possible?"

"That's the idea. A small fishing boat, maybe."

"You wish to have such a boat?"

"I'm considering the idea, Juan."

"For to escape with?"

"Yeah."

"I will find this boat for you, *Señor* Bolan. At the price you say."

Bolan dug inside his shirt and through the skinsuit to the chamois money belt at his waist. His Vegas "winnings" were secure and dry there. He worked several bills free and handed them over.

"Do what you can with this," he said.

"Thousand dollar bills," Juan observed in a hushed voice. "They are real?"

"Genuine Grover Clevelands," Bolan assured him. "Liberated from occupied Vegas just last night. Don't worry, it's cool money. Can you spend it without attracting the wrong kind of attention?"

The kid was dazed by the sudden wealth in his hand. "I would spend it at the very gates of hell," he muttered.

"Okay, but be very careful. Get the best deal you can on the boat and keep the change for yourself. How—?"

"I could not keep your money, Mack Bolan."

"The hell you could not. Call it a birthday present from me to the kid, if you'd rather."

"But I will need less than half—"

"The better for the kid," Bolan said brusquely. "Shut up about that and listen to me, Juan. I don't want anything new or *tourista* looking. Understand? I want something old and decrepit looking, but seaworthy and with enough fuel reserves to at least island-hop."

"Island hop?"

"You know . . . travel from island to island."

"Oh, yes. A diesel would be better."

"I leave that to you. But find someone you can personally trust—that is, if you have any choice. If not, then do the best you can and leave the rest to me."

"I must be very quiet with this," the boy reflected.

81

"Very."

"I think I know the right man. Do not worry, *Señor* Bolan. I *will find* the right man."

Bolan grinned. "I thought you were going to call me Mack."

"A-OK, Mack. I will leave right away."

"Take Rosalita."

"*Señor?*"

"Take Rosalita with you. Stay gone until this mess blows over. Is there some place you can take her for a couple of days?"

"We have family in Puerta Vista," the boy replied. "But. . . ."

"Then do it. Take her there *first*. Evita, also. Then make the arrangements for the boat."

"Okay yes, and I will then return—"

"No, don't come back here. Chances are I'll be slipping out shortly behind you. Let's go talk to Evita and work out a time and place for a meet. Then you get those women away from here."

That was the plan.

It did not work out quite that way, however.

Evita adamantly refused to even consider the suggestion that she accompany Juan and Rosalita to Puerta Vista. "You will need me to get you through the police lines," she told Bolan. "I stay with you, and that is final."

So it was final. Bolan shrugged his shoulders and walked to the truck with the kids.

"Take care," he instructed Juan. His eyes warmed on the girl, and he added, "Guard your treasures, Juan."

The youth solemnly nodded his head and translated the parting words for his wife's understanding. She did the thing with her eyes, and she brushed Bolan's cheek with her lips as he helped her into the vehicle.

"Good luck," she whispered, in perhaps the only *Inglisa* at her command.

He watched the departing truck until it was out of sight, realizing that friendship was a quality of caring—not a duration of acquaintance. Bolan *cared.* And he wanted those kids out of his shadow of death. The girl had understood this. She, apparently, had cared also.

He entered the cabin to the sound of water running into the bathtub. A dainty pile of feminine things was on a chair just outside the curtain. He could see the shadowy outline of Evita the Woman bending over the tub and it was quite an outline.

The noise from the plumbing chugged to a halt. The lovely Spanish-Borinquen head appeared over the top of the curtain. "*Excusame*," she sang out. "*Una momento, por favor*, while I scrub away Glass Bay."

Bolan snatched up a primed Thompson and made a strategic retreat.

It was time for another recon, anyway. He went to the high ground and prowled about for a few minutes, then he sat down with his back against a tree and lit a cigarette.

How long had it been since he'd slept? Two weeks? Three? It seemed that long. A guy on his last mile of life could pack a lot of living into a single day. Barely more than twenty-four hours earlier, Bolan had risen from a bed in Las Vegas and gone out to test the odds against him on Sudden Death Strip. And what a hell of a time it had been. And now here he was in Puerto Rico, of all damn places. Bone weary, emotionally exhausted, scared out of his Goddamned skull. How many men, he vaguely wondered, had he killed this week? Fifty? A hundred? Two hundred?

The odds had to catch up sooner or later. Why not sooner? Why not right here, in Puerto Rico, at 20 degrees north latitude. Wasn't that the equatorial parallel which had given birth and first breath to *The Executioner*? Sure, sure, that was where the monster was born—at 20 degress north, not at Pittsfield. The Mafia hadn't been the midwife, but Life itself. The Executioner had been born to Mom Nature. Dad Society had knocked her up—and along came Bolan the Bold, a breech birth, a monster in military cloth. Pittsfield merely represented the inevitable coming-of-age for this bastard child nobody wanted. The Executioner.

How many men had he killed this week?

Bolan sighed and got to his feet.

Not enough.

But that was enough self-pity to last for several weeks. He crushed out the cigarette, called out his energy reserves, straightened himself up, and went back down the hill to the cabin.

Evita was standing at the kitchen sink, peering into the only mirror in the place, and brushing out the shiney raven hair.

And she wasn't wearing a goddamned thing.

Bolan set the Thompson against the wall and told her, gruffly, "You can't get away with that."

Her eyes met his in the mirror. She replied, mimicking his gruffness, "Who says I wish to get away with it?"

If that tiny nipped waist was her equatorial zone, then she owned one hell of an interesting. ...

84

"20 degrees *south* latitude," he mumbled. "That's a swinging parallel, Evita."

She wrinkled her nose at him in the mirror. "Take your bath," she commanded. "You also have the stink of Glass Bay."

The stink he had, Bolan thought, would never yield to mere soap and water. But he smiled and began undressing. Maybe at least he could wash away an accumulated film of self pity.

That 20th parallel south had already taken care of his fatigue problem. He had that certain feeling, though, that it was going to greatly add to it in just a very little while.

How many beautiful women had he loved this week?

Not enough.

And that wasn't self pity talking.

Bolan was still living to the point.

7: FAIRYLAND

He slung her over his shoulder, carried her up the ladder to the loft and placed her gently on the feather mattress. Then he sat cross-legged beside her, as he silently contemplated the loveliness of this very unlikely cop.

Her eyes were warmly alive and aware as they slid slowly along his nudity. "You are beautiful, for a caveman," she whispered.

His gaze wavered and turned away. "This isn't a required part of the game plan, you know. We could skip it."

She laughed softly but did not quite manage to make it sound light and humorous as she replied, "*Now* he tells me. Too late, *querido*. It is very much required at this point."

He reached for her, his hand finding the incredibly velvet softness of the shiny little belly. A forefinger delicately traced the outline of the naval depression and he said, "Those kids, Juan and Rosalita. . . . I wonder if they realize how great they really have it."

Her manner abruptly changed. She removed his hand and turned toward the wall.

He said, "Hell, Evita, I didn't mean. . . ."

"You did not mean a comparison, I know," she

replied in a muffled tone. "Just the same it is there, and I know this. I am three months in a Mafia bed. This morning I did not know Mack Bolan. This evening I am in *his* bed. Yes, it is a harsh comparison. Much too harsh. So throw me back to the Mafia, Mack Bolan."

"How many men have you loved this week, Evita?"

Her shoulder twitched and she said, "Loved? I have not loved."

"And I have not murdered," he told her.

She turned slowly to look at him. "What does this mean?"

"We're pro's, Evita. We make war, *not love, not murder*. That's all it means. When I mentioned Juan and Rosalita I was only thinking of that very innocent and special fairyland that you and I have left forever. Would you like to trade places with Rosalita, Eve? Would you, if you could?"

She moved her head in a slow negative, her eyes pinned to Bolan's. "Would you like it better if I did?"

He grinned and shook his head. "I wouldn't know what to do with a Rosalita."

"You call me Eve," she whispered. "Do you know what to do with an Eve?"

"The original Eve wanted truth," he reminded her. "She picked the forbidden fruit of knowledge."

"Yes?"

"Yes."

"And found love?"

He shook his head again, soberly. "She found war. And hell. And damnation. And eviction from fairyland."

"Adam, also? He found all this?"

"Yes."

"They were fools, this Adam and Eve," she declared bitterly.

"Where would this world be, Evita," he quietly asked her, "without fools like these?"

She understood. "Thank you," she said huskily.

He gathered her into his arms and pulled her close. "I left out the most important point of the story," he said.

Her arms went tightly about his neck and she clung to him. Her breathing was a bit ragged and he had the taste of tears on his lips as she said, "You did?"

"Yes," he replied, finding a bit of difficulty with his own breathing. "Through it all, Adam and Eve found each other."

"Oh *Dios*, Mack!" she cried. "Find *me*, please find me!"

He found her, and was glad, understanding in that jarring moment of truth that each had desperately needed to find the other at just that point in time and space.

Even a couple of war-hardened pro's needed a trip through fairyland from time to time.

The war faded, hell wavered, and even damnation lost its sting as Bolan and the law traded points of reality, and merged them, and expanded them into that all-consuming flame which is known only to those who live largely, love largely, and fully expect to die in the same manner.

For those who live to the point, Bolan decided, there are very special rewards.

The sun had become quite low in the sky when

Bolan stirred and gently disentangled himself from that sweet press.

"Let us die here now, like this," Evita murmured lazily.

"We just might," he told her. He rubbed her thigh and said, "Come on, rise and shine, time to hit the firing line. The enemy could have brought a battalion in here on us and we'd have never known it."

"I have been listening to your heart beat," she said, "in all the world there has been no other sound. The war drums have fallen silent. Anyway, the battalions would never find us here."

"Don't be too sure of that." He rolled onto his knees and knelt there for a moment, studying her. Then he smiled and said, "I like this hat."

"*Sombrero? Por la cabeza?*—the head? I do not wear the hat."

"Figure of speech," he explained. "*Por la senorita de amor.*"

Her eyes glowed at him and she replied, "Yes, I also like this hat."

"Let's put the other one back on for a minute," Bolan suggested, regretfully. "You told me that Triesta overheard you making a phone call."

"This is true."

"It was an official call?"

"Official, yes. I was reporting the events at Glass Bay."

"In English?"

Her eyes fell. "Yes."

"Why not in Spanish? You said it's the official language here. Wouldn't it have been safer to use the native tongue? Did Triesta know Spanish?"

"The man ... my contact ... he does not know Spanish."

90

Bolan sighed. "I'd feel much better, Evita, if you'd level with me. The whole story."

She sighed also. "Some things, Mack Bolan, I can not. . . ."

"No games," he said firmly. "I have to know."

The interrogation was becoming an ordeal for Evita. "You have heard . . . the expression . . . *strike force?*"

He nodded. "Feds. Does Washington have men here?"

She hesitated, then replied, "Yes. Officially, these are special advisors. At the moment their greatest concern seems to be for . . . for Mack Bolan."

"I see," he said quietly.

"They were expecting you in Puerto Rico."

"And you confirmed their expectations."

"Yes. I told them you had arrived."

"And this is the conversation Triesta overheard?"

"Yes."

"Okay, so what was the game plan from that point?"

"I was to report back . . . when you were dead."

"What else?"

"As insurance . . . in case you should break free . . . a containment network would be established."

"Uh huh. This is the police line you mentioned?"

"Yes. Their only interest is Mack Bolan." She said it with a sigh. "They do not wish to show their hand at Glass Bay. Not yet. Too much work has gone into. . . ."

He said, "All right, I have the picture. Now let's talk about the lady cop. What was your Mack Bolan assignment?"

"None, but to report your death. Or your escape."

91

"And everything between you and me has been strictly on the level."

"This I swear, yes."

He said, "Okay, I believe you. Now. Other than the headhunters, exactly what is waiting for me out there, Evita?"

She shrugged daintily. "I do not know. I know only that they are very determined that you die in Puerto Rico."

"Yeah, I got the same reception in Vegas," Bolan muttered. "The Bolan kill is on. They don't even want me in court. They just want me dead."

"They?"

"The feds. The political heat is on."

"This is not just," she whispered.

"Sure it is," he told her. "Nobody gave me a hunting license." He shrugged. "A guy takes his ride and pays his fare. It makes no sense to scream about the high cost of riding. Anyway, this is the way I want it. I don't want a free ride. That would make me just another contract killer."

"You are a man unique," Evita murmured.

"I am a man realistic," Bolan argued. He smiled. "Don't forget Adam and Eve. If they hadn't paid their fare the world would have seen nothing more than a population explosion of hairless apes. The human race is more than a tribe of naked apes, Evita."

"That is most profound," she commented, eyes sparkling.

He kissed her, with tenderness, and then he quickly went down the ladder and began getting into his clothing.

Evita followed a moment later, as he was harnessing into the Beretta's sideleather. She watched him briefly, warmly, then she sighed and began rounding up her own things.

Bolan grabbed her from behind and kissed her again, then he picked up a Thompson and went outside, clad only in the black skinsuit.

The sun was setting at 20 degrees north latitude.

He stood quietly on the high ground for a couple of minutes and watched the surrounding countryside and thought of Evita while his ears tuned themselves to the sounds of the land.

She was a hell of a gal. The name itself was the Spanish diminutive for Eve. Little Eve. Not her, hell no. *Big* Eve. Very soon now he would be saying goodbye ... to this land, to this woman, to the eternal part of himself which he would be leaving there.

Yes, there were rewards for living large.

There were also heavy taxes.

He thought of another Big Eve, a Cuban lady soldier he'd met and left forever at Miami Beach ... large Margarita. She had died large at Miami Beach, and she'd left a hell of a large marker in the memory of Mack Bolan.

He remembered her stirring poetry, also ... stirring for a guy in Bolan's shoes.

"The world dies 'twixt every heartbeat,
and is born again
in each new perception of the mind."

Yeah. Right on, Margarita.

"For each of us
the order of life is to *perceive* and *perish*
and *perceive* again."

The *battle* order, Margarita. Life is a battle, from womb to grave, if there is any meaning to it at all.

"And who can say which is which—

93

for every human experience builds a new
world
    in its own image—
and death itself is but an unusual perception."

Right on, little *soldada*.

You too, Evita, little *policia*, right the hell on.

He left the hill and circled to the far side of the
cabin, continuing the soft recon. Another twenty
minutes and it would be dark enough to move out, to
keep the rendezvous with Juan Escadrillo, and to go
on to the next horsie of the carousel.

He stopped to inspect the jeep, then stiffened
suddenly and released the safety on the Thompson.
A vehicle was coming along that road.

Bolan threw a quick look toward the cabin, then
stepped into the timber and moved swiftly along a
parallel course with the roadway.

The Executioner felt another unusual perception
coming on.

It was, he knew, time to go out of fairyland.

8: THE CHOICE

It was a Chevy, one of the small economy models, about two years old, and it was carrying a fresh accumulation of plateau dust. It also carried four men, each of whom seemed very much out of place on this Puerto Rico back-road.

They were total strangers to Bolan. They were also, he quickly deduced, strangers to the land. The vehicle had come to a quick halt at first sight of the cabin, then quietly reversed its track and came to rest around a bend in the road.

All four men stepped outside and stood conversing across the roof of the vehicle. They spoke quietly, too softly for Bolan's ears to pick up more than a word here and there—but definitely English words.

The car was radio equipped. One of the men leaned inside and said something into a mike. A responsive squawk from the radio receiver confirmed that English was the language in use, but again without sufficient clarity for Bolan's understanding.

The problem, from Bolan's standpoint, was the question of identification. If the guys were cops, he could simply fade out. Evita would be left in good hands and Bolan himself would be in no worse shape than at any time since he'd hit the island.

If they were not cops though . . . .

One of the men was pulling a sawed-off shotgun from the rear seat. Another was spinning the cylinder of a heavy revolver and checking the load. The guy at the radio swung back to the outside and passed a soft command to the others.

They split up.

One remained with the vehicle. Another advanced along the road toward the cabin. The other two went to opposite sides and disappeared into the brush.

They were closing on the house.

Bolan would have preferred to take them while they were bunched up. If the guys turned out to be some of Lavagni's scouts, there could be hell to pay now. A guy on the short end of the odds could not afford to allow such a situation to get out of his direct control.

Bolan had done so.

But there was that nagging question of identification . . . another of the built-in handicaps to the Executioner's war effort.

He moved on deeper and circled back for an approach from the rear, then he stepped onto the road and came in with the fiery red sun setting directly behind him.

The guy was leaning against the car, his attention focused in the direction of the house, when the quiet jungle cat moved in behind him and the heavy steel muzzle of the Thompson dug into his spine.

He stiffened, and froze there, and Bolan could almost feel the tumbling energies of that suddenly electified mind.

"Okay, okay," the guy said, in a voice with all the moisture suddenly gone out of it. "Don't, for God's sake."

It was a matter of blind reaction versus conditioned instincts, and Bolan had his identification. The guy was no American federal cop; he was no kind of cop.

Without wasting another precious second of time, Bolan whipped the stock of the heavy gun up and against the back of the soldier's skull in a lashing slap. The guy crumbled without a sound and sprawled face down in the dust. Bolan turned him over and gave him another vicious jab to the throat, then he stepped over the lifeless remains and hurried on along the road toward the cabin.

Big Eve was alone up there and definitely not about to fall into good hands.

The one with the shotgun was moving into the yard as Bolan rounded the bend, another was stepping out of the bushes to the right.

The front door to the cabin was standing open, and he saw a flash of motion across that open doorway.

"Hold it!" Bolan yelled, more for Evita's benefit than for anything else.

The guy in front whirled, bringing the shotgun around with him, and the Thompson's opening argument caught him in mid-turn and laid him down in a convulsive sideways sprawl. The shotgun boomed, sending its double-oughts spraying harmlessly into the air.

And then Evita was standing there in that doorway, clad only in a bra and a half-slip, and a Thompson was in her arms.

She screamed, "Mack!" as her chopper erupted, the fire going toward a point on Bolan's blind left side.

The weapon was too much for her and she was

fighting to keep that bucking muzzle down, but to no avail. Her fire-track was a chaotic sweep skyward —but it was evidently scarey enough to send her target diving for cover after one wild shot at Bolan.

Meanwhile the guy on the right had gone for Evita. He was running across the yard and firing from the hip, the heavy slugs from the revolver chewing up the doorjamb behind her.

Living large, a lot of life could be packed into a single second.

And a lot of death.

All of the foregoing had been playing upon the background of Bolan's consciousness, reeling out in frozen sequences of peripheral awareness; perhaps, he reflected later, it was the awareness of that submerged human side of man-in-combat.

From the moment of first blood, however, back at the vehicle, Bolan's single overriding consideration was for the safety of Evita Aguilar, Big Eve. The combat order was as single-minded, and the panoramic action outside that cabin was telescoped into a single moment in time and as a continuous movement in attack-mode.

His first burst caught the front man and sent him beyond the lens of that mental telescope. The second burst unfalteringly found its track onto the gunner at the right, and the guy's last couple of rounds toward Evita were probably no more than the dying reflex of his trigger-finger. He was stopped in midstride and punched back for several yards loss before touching down—and already Bolan was swinging into the threat from the left.

The guy over there was diving away from that harmless confrontation with Evita's Thompson, and Bolan's next burst added measurably to that move-

98

ment, sending the guy into a somersaulting roll into the bushes.

A snap-glance toward the cabin assured Bolan that the girl was okay. He went quickly from body to body, verifying the results, then he slung the heated Thompson across his back and went to the woman.

Her eyes were wild but exhilarated as she let the heavy weapon droop and then fall to the steps. She crumbled into his arms and he pulled her in close.

"You okay?" he asked anxiously.

"Yes, yes, okay," she panted.

"You were great," he told her.

"Great, no. Out of mind, yes. Why would anyone build a *loco* gun such as this one?"

Bolan strangled off a chuckle as his fingers encountered the unmistakable sticky warmth of blood. "You're hit," he announced calmly, and spun her about for inspection.

"It was like a sting of the bee," she said raggedly. "It is nothing?"

He grunted and replied, "Well, almost nothing. But you'll have a souvenir to show your grandchildren."

A .38 slug had plowed a shallow furrow along the soft underside of her left arm, just below the armpit. Another inch toward center and it would have been a fatal wound. By such insignificant dimensions of mass were the measurements of life and death.

He pulled her into the cabin and quickly washed the wound with soap and water, then he applied a disinfectant from the kitchen cupboard and bound the arm with gauze.

"We have to hurry," he said tightly.

"I am all right," she assured him.

"Okay, get your clothes on. Those guys are part of a coordinated sweep."

Evita nodded her understanding and finished dressing, wrinkling her nose at the torn blouse. "I put back on the stink of Glass Bay," she commented lightly.

Bolan did also, hastily donning the slacks and shirt he had worn there. Then he told the woman, "Go through this place with a fine comb. Make sure there's nothing left behind to show I've been here."

He started for the door but she reached out and stopped him, laying her cheek against his chest and encircling him with her arms.

Bolan said gruffly, "It'll be okay."

"Mack, I . . . all this death. It does not bother you?"

Of course it bothered him. He told her, "How much choice is there, Evita?"

She shivered and lifted the troubled face to peer into his eyes. "I am just now realize . . . this terror, this bloody struggle . . . it is all of your life. It is never ending, is it? I can give you a choice, Mack. Surrender to me. Go with me to San Juan. I promise you, there is feeling for you in this commonwealth. I have friends, high friends. I will fight to keep you in Puerto Rico."

Bolan sighed and told her, "You're not thinking straight, Evita. First item, you told me yourself that the law wants me dead in Puerto Rico. I'd never see the inside of a police station. Second—"

"I will guarantee you differently!" she cried. "I swear!"

"All right, even if you could guarantee something like that—I've never heard of a jail or a prison that was secure against the reach of the mob. They'd

100

love nothing better than to have me boxed in and defenseless, and they *would* get to me, Evita."

"There could be designed a suitable protection," she replied stubbornly.

Bolan shook his head. "Not a chance. As for keeping me in Puerto Rico, I am wanted for capital crimes in a dozen states and two foreign countries, not to mention that I'm an army deserter and also top man on the FBI's list. Assuming that I could get tried and released in all those places, which would be a wonder equalled only by the second coming of Christ, I would still have years of court battles to look forward to, and with Johnny Matthew dogging me every step of the way."

"Who is this Johnny Matthew?"

"The non-existent Mafia," he said whimsically. "If you're wondering about my chances with legal justice, just consider that weird fact. The mighty U.S. government has backed down to the point of using a cover name when referring to *Mafiosi*. They are Johnny Matthew now."

"Yes, I have heard of this timidity," she said quietly. "It is shameful."

"Anyway," he added, smiling soberly, "I am not ready to throw down my gun and walk peacefully away. I'm my own Pentagon now, my own war department, and my own executive branch of government. I make the decisions and I carry them out. And it's war, Evita. War to the bloody end."

"It is your choice," she murmured, taking a wooden step backwards.

"It's no choice at all," Bolan told her. "It's the only way to go."

He spun away from her and went outside.

When Evita joined him there moments later, the

jeep had been pulled into the yard and the three bodies were piled into the rear. Bolan was carefully collecting the ejected shells from the Thompsons. She helped him round up the fallen enemy weapons, and these were added to the collection in the jeep.

"What is your plan?" she asked him.

"I'm taking this load of garbage out of here," he replied. "There's a car just up the lane, also another dead soldier. I'll pick him up, and you follow me out in their car."

"We will abandon the jeep?"

"That's the idea. I noticed a strip-mine up along the foothills. Do you know the place?"

She nodded. "It is Aggregates Limited. About three miles from here."

"Okay, then I'll follow you. Come on, let's hit it. Too much delay already."

Bolan drove her to the other vehicle, where he picked up the fourth body and gave Evita a snub nosed .32 from the shoulder holster of the first victim.

"This one I can handle," she assured him, spinning the cylinder with an expert touch.

He said, "I'll bet you can," and went to inspect the Chevy.

She followed close on his heels and announced, "It is a Glass Bay company car. But something has been added."

"The radio?"

"No." She ran a hand across the top of the car. "This."

She was pointing out a peculiar design on the roof. Four circular plastic decals were placed along the centerline, each colored a bright orange. Bolan

102

had noted the design earlier, but had thought nothing of it.

"That's new, eh?" he mused.

"Yes. It is new since this morning."

"Air spotters," he muttered.

"What?"

"It's for visual identification from the air."

"The helicopters," Evita decided. "They have been added to the hunt, no? But it will be night very shortly. The marks and the helicopters will mean nothing in the night."

Bolan said, "These will. That's luminescent paint."

"We can peel them off."

"No," he replied quickly. "We leave them on. This can be turned to our advantage. Listen, Evita, you'll have to drive the jeep. I hate to put you in charge of a hearse, but—"

He was interrupted by the squawking of the radio inside the Chevy, as a testy New England accent swelled in from a noisy background to demand, "Ground Four, Ground Four, what have you got? Report, dammit!"

Evita was counting the four decals atop the car with exaggerated stabs of a forefinger. "I believe you are being paged," she said.

Bolan grinned and leaned in for the microphone. "That's a chopper," he told her. "I could hear the rotors in the background."

He thumbed the mike into transmit mode and put on his street voice. "Ground Four," he announced casually. "Nothing here. Another farm shanty. It's clean."

"Air One, okay," came the noisy reply. "But stay close to the damn radio, eh? Go on to the next checkpoint."

Bolan was gambling. He showed Evita crossed fingers and thumbed on the transmitter again. "Bullshit," he snarled. "It's damn near dark and all we've done so far is roust a bunch of peasants. I say we're wasting it."

"So you got something brighter in mind?" was the response from the chopper.

"Yeh, and I can see it from here," Bolan's street voice replied. "There's a strip mine just up into the hills. Can you see it?"

"Air one, naw, we're running the beach right now. You got a feeling about that place?"

"I got so much feeling I'm getting hard," Bolan reported.

The guy in the helicopter chuckled and said, "Okay, follow your needle, tiger. Call in as soon as you get up there."

"Ground Four, right, you'll be the first to know."

Bolan threw the mike onto the dashboard and turned a worried face to the girl. "Well now we'll see," he told her.

"That was very clever, learning his position," Evita commented. "You act very well, Mack Bolan. You could have made it in Hollywood."

He grinned and said, "Yeah, just another wasted life. Where did Mack Bolan go wrong, eh?"

"More men should be so wrong," Evita said soberly, then the she spun about and marched to the jeep, climbing in without a glance at the cargo behind her.

Bolan sighed and slid into the Chevy.

Yeah, already Fairyland was far behind them. Big Eve knew it. And she'd found another corner of hell to hang her hat on.

So had Bolan. He was about out of ammo for the

104

Thompsons—and they were hardly worth the trouble of dragging around. With a coordinated air-ground search by Lavagni plus the unknown quality of police threat awaiting him at Puerta Vista, the gauntlet seemed to be shrinking in around him.

The jeep pulled up beside him and the girl showed him a tense smile. "I want you to know," she said, "that I agree with your choice. Perhaps I am the bad cop. But I must follow my conscience. And my conscience tells me that the good cop would help you, Mack Bolan, not conspire for your death."

Bolan said, "Thanks. I like this hat too, Eve."

Her smile brightened then abruptly disappeared, and the jeep leapt forward.

Bolan see-sawed the Chevy into the turnaround and plowed on after her.

Yeah, she'd found a new corner of hell, all right.

Where had Mack Bolan gone wrong?

Somewhere between hell and paradise, in a lost corner of that great jungle called life.

And he absolutely would not have had it any other way.

9: PAYDIRT

They arrived at the mining site in the waning moments of twilight and Bolan drove the Chevy right through the flimsy gate. Evita swung in behind him and they proceeded along the dusty road to a lip overlooking the ugly white gash in the mountainside.

He parked on the overlook and scrambled out for a quick recon of the area. Heavy equipment stood idle here and there along the strip. No lights were showing and there was no evidence of a watchman.

Evita joined him at the front bumper of the jeep and told him, "The spot is perfect. Send them over from here. They would not be discovered until morning."

He replied, "No, let's get all the mileage out of this thing we can. Listen ... I can handle what needs to be done here." He pointed to a small building, constructed of cement blocks and snuggled into the lee of the mountain a few hundred feet downrange. "That should be their explosives storage. Shoot the lock off if you have to but get inside there, Evita. Look for dynamite, in sticks. Get me four or five. And pick up blasting caps, fuses, you know."

She said, "Yes, I know," and took off on a run for the blockhouse.

Bolan swung about to the rear of the vehicle and started dragging out bodies. One of them he placed in the driver's seat and slumped him over the steering wheel. The others he scattered about the landscape and placed weapons in or near their hands.

Then he returned to the vehicles and went to work on the Thompsons, specifically on the ammo drums. Between the bunch, he hoped to be able to come up with at least enough of the heavy .45's to reload one drum almost to capacity.

By the time Evita returned from her errand, panting but glowing with success, Bolan had his stage set and he was ready for the next big gamble.

He kissed her, sat her down on the ground and brushed the dust from her nose. "Okay," he said. "Now here is what we are going to try."

Charlie Dragone was seated irritably in the transparent bubble of "Air One" and closely watching the rocky shoreline as it slipped past several hundred feet beneath him. He pressed the throat-mike and asked the pilot, "How're we doing on fuel?"

"About ten minutes left," Jack Grimaldi replied. "For all the good we're doing, we might as well—"

"Shut up!" Dragone snarled.

They had hit it off wrong from the very start. Dragone did not like wise-guy nobodies who didn't know their place.

He punched in the radio command channel and said, "Air One to Ground Control. It's almost dark and it's been nothing but zip. Whatta you think? Do we keep it up?"

Quick Tony Lavagni's voice returned immediately, vibrating excitedly into the earphones. "I was just about to give you a call, Charlie. Listen, I think I got something going down here on the waterfront. See if you can reach Latigo and tell 'im to close on Puerta Vista."

Latigo was in Air Two, screening the west side of Glass Bay and out of radio range of the east side surface vehicles.

Dragone replied, "You mean him and all his ground scouts?"

"Yeh, let's get 'em all together. At least headed this way."

The chief triggerman acknowledged the instructions, then he punched into the other communications channel and relayed the word to Earl Latigo in Air Two.

This had hardly been accomplished when an excited voice swirled in faintly on the air-to-ground net. "Air One, Air One, can you hear me?"

Dragone busily punched his transmitter into that channel to reply, "Yeah, I hear you. Who's this?"

"Ground Four. And shit man I hit it!"

"You hit what? Talk straight out, buster!"

"Ass, man, ass! It's in a jeep and full of juice!"

"This is Ground Four? Where are you? At that mine?"

"Yeah. Get it up here, eh?"

"Well wait a minute! Are you sure? The boss thinks he's got something, too, down here on the coast. I'm sending all the cars his way!"

"Great, you do that," replied the exultant voice. "I don't need no help anyway. I got this guy boxed in tight, and man his juice is all mine!"

"Well now wait a minute!" Dragone cried.

"Ground Four out, and don't bother calling for awhile. I'm gonna be busy."

"I said wait a minute, dammit!"

There was no response.

The future right hand of a future *Capo* threw a perplexed glance toward his pilot and muttered, "Goddammit, feast or famine! How the hell do you like that?"

Grimaldi was searching his chart. He pressed his throat mike and said, "I've got the place. There's just about enough gas to run up and look, if you'd like."

"I dunno," Dragone muttered. He punched the channel selector again and tried to raise Lavagni, without success. "I wish people would stay at their goddamn radios," he complained.

"Do we go or don't we?" the pilot wanted to know. "Make up your mind while we have some light left. I can't pick up landmarks in the dark."

"We got enough gas for the round trip?"

"I told you I did," Grimaldi replied. "But if you're going to dick around all night thinking about—"

"Awright, go," Dragone growled.

As it turned out, they had more gas than light. The final minute of travel was conducted during that transition period between sunset and moonrise, and they arrived over the site with no light at all, except for that being provided by the vehicle with the four glowing markers on its roof.

The headlamps were at full blaze, the path of brilliance revealing a jeep swerved and tilted onto a lip of mountainside above the gaping slit trench. A couple of bodies could be seen sprawled out behind the jeep, and a still figure was slumped over the wheel.

And nothing at all seemed to be moving down there.

In a voice thick with emotion, Dragone declared, "By God I believe it's paydirt, all right."

"Do I take her down?" Grimaldi asked.

"Wait a minute." The triggerman pressed the throat mike and said, "Ground Four, what's the situation down there?"

There was no response.

He tried again. "Ground Four, goddammit, report! Whatta you got there?"

A feeble reply came back. "I'm hit."

"Did you get him?"

"Sure ... can't you see? But I'm ... hit ... bad. Can't move."

Grimaldi turned on the ground floods and dropped to about fifty feet, washing the scene in a pale glow of light.

"Yeah," he breathed into the intercom, "that's paydirt."

"Okay, take it on down," Dragone instructed.

The helicopter settled to the ground at about midpoint between the two automobiles.

Dragone growled, "Cover me." He scrambled outside and made a cautious advance on the jeep, remaining clear of the lights from the company car as long as possible, his revolver extended in the firing position and ready to roar.

As he drew abreast of the little vehicle, he fired two deliverate shots into the slumped figure at the wheel, taking no chances whatever that a feeble spark of life there would flare up to turn his victory sour. Then he lunged forward, grabbed the corpse by the hair of the head, and swiveled that lifeless face into the light.

And then Charlie Dragone turned suddenly very

111

cold and very stiff, very strongly aware that he had made his life's final blunder.

There would be no sitting in state at the right hand of a *Capo*—no basking in unlimited wealth and influence and power—there would be nothing again ever for Charlie Dragone.

He looked up and into the headlamps of the company car, and his face showed the total resignation, that smashing finality of utter defeat—and probably Dragone never heard the growling chatter of the Thompson submachine gun that ripped him, sieved him, and flung him over the edge of the overlook and into the pits of Aggregates Limited.

Several yards away, one accomplished and versatile Mafia flyer had also become aware of the new turn of events—a turn which somehow seemed entirely too familiar.

He was trying to breathe past the muzzle pressure of a very business-like .32 revolver and watching the tall man with the Thompson walk casually toward his aircraft.

"Oh God, no!" Grimaldi groaned. "Not again!"

A coldly decisive female voice with a soft Spanish slur told him, "But yes. And do not dare to even swallow the spit until I say that you may."

And then Bolan was there, and spinning him around, and shoving him back to the aircraft.

No words were spoken until all three were inside and secured into the harnesses, then the big cold bastard asked him, "How much do you want to go on living, Grimaldi?"

"Just tell me where you want to go," the pilot replied, sighing. "But I think you ought to start paying my salary."

The guy actually grinned at the stab of humor

112

and told him, "I just might." The grin disappeared abruptly and the face turned again to ice and Bolan commanded, "Lift her off."

Grimaldi lifted her off, and heeled her about, and pointed her nose toward the coast.

Yes, definitely, the whole scene was entirely too familiar.

"You're too much, Bolan," the flying *Mafioso* announced into the intercom. "I'll bet you sprinkle gunpowder on your Wheaties."

"I take it where I can get it," the laconic bastard replied.

Grimaldi knew better. This guy moved it to wherever he thought he could take it. And now he was moving it to Puerta Vista. But Grimaldi was betting that he knew something about Puerta Vista that Bolan didn't know.

He told his hi-jacker, "We might not have enough fuel. It's marginal at best."

Bolan growled back, "You'd better get it there, Jack. Your life is on the same margin."

Grimaldi did not doubt that for a moment. He shrugged and replied, "So I'll get it there if I have to pee in the tank."

Hell yes. Grimaldi would get it there if he had to *bleed* in it.

He wanted in the worse way to deliver Bolan to Puerta Vista.

With every gun on the island closing at this very moment on that tiny fishing village, Grimaldi could think of no better place to drop Mack Bolan.

It could mean paydirt yet. It could mean, hell, riches beyond Jack Grimaldi's wildest dreams.

"I'll get you there," he assured his passengers.

And then Earl Latigo's voice was crackling into

113

the earphones. "Air One from Air Two. Where are you? What's going on?"

The cold voice in the intercom instructed Grimaldi, "Very carefully, Jack. Tell him what happened, with one exception. Bolan is dead, also. You are returning alone. Carefully now, soldier."

That impressive black Beretta with the muzzle silencer appeared in Grimaldi's peripheral vision and the barrel made a small indentation alongside the throat mike.

Grimaldi sighed and punched into the command channel. "Air One," he said tiredly. "Good news and bad. Charlie got Bolan. But he didn't live to brag about it. I'm coming in empty."

Bolan nodded approvingly and Latigo's elated tones swirled back with, "Hell, I'd about given it up! He really got the bastard? Bolan's dead? Where'd you nail him?"

"Up in the hills. I, uh, don't feel much like talking right now, Earl. Tell you all about it when we get together."

"I guess that's why I can't raise Tony," Air Two replied.

Bolan growled, "Send them home."

Grimaldi sighed again, heavily. "Boss wants you back at the joint," he told Latigo. "Go on home, Earl."

"My ground crews too?"

The Great Stone Face nodded his head.

Grimaldi pressed the throat mike and said, "Yeah, everybody is heading in."

"Okay, see you there," Air Two replied, signing off.

Bolan eased off the pressure of the Beretta and

114

commented, "I might even pay you a salary plus bonuses, Jack."

That, thought Grimaldi, was because the guy didn't know what he was heading into. Quick Tony couldn't be reached on the radio because he was setting up something at Puerta Vista.

He went along with the gag, though, and told Bolan, "When Tony hears about this, you'd better make it enough to get me to Lower Slobbovia, eh."

Bolan did not reply, and they went on in silence until the lights of Puerta Vista became visible.

Then the woman spoke, for the first time since entering the 'copter. "Circle from the east," she instructed him. "On the first road north of the coastal highway, just inside the village, you will see the church. It has a high bell tower. You will land in the churchyard to the rear."

Grimaldi nodded his head and glanced at the ice man. "Is that what you want, Mr. Bolan?"

"You heard the lady," Bolan replied. "Do it."

He found the spot with no trouble at all, and he set her down without landing lights exactly where the lady wanted, and with hardly a bump.

The moon was coming up, and visibility was definitely improving. Grimaldi shivered, wondering what was coming up next—and fearing the worst.

He cut the engine and the rotors were still chugging around in the rundown spin when the big guy started battering the radio with his pistol and ripping out the ignition system.

Then Bolan grabbed Grimaldi and hauled him to the ground and told him, "Run east, soldier. Don't slow down, and don't look back."

Grimaldi had absolutely no desire to argue with the man. Paydirt now meant simply remaining alive.

He started running, mentally bracing himself for the shot in the back which never came.

Twice in one day the bastard had let him off. Jack Grimaldi simply could not understand it. He ran on, almost hoping that the big guy would make it through Puerta Vista in one piece. Maybe the guy wasn't such a total bastard, after all.

It was a dumb hope, though. Grimaldi was the lucky one. He was running out of Puerta Vista.

Bolan was striding into it. Straight into Quick Tony's paydirt.

10: SOFT SELL

During those tense moments at the strip mine, while awaiting the arrival of the helicopter, Bolan and Evita performed reluctant farewells, both aware that this might be their last opportunity to do so. And when all the words of appreciation and mutual admiration had been said, she asked him, "What will you do upon leaving Puerto Rico?"

He reflected on the question for a moment, then replied, "I had planned to chase the brass ring but ... well, I guess it's best that I tuck my tail in and make a run for home ground."

She nodded her head in agreement. "This would be best. You do not now think it wise to enter the tournament, yes?"

"I don't like the focus the thing has taken," Bolan explained. "Anything I go for now will likely be just another setup, and I'll be fighting their war their way."

"This is not good."

"No, it isn't. I'll have to pull back and hope for another try another day. My way, and on my terms. If we can capture this chopper, we'll go on into Puerta Vista. We'll make the meet with Juan. Then you will go your way and I will go mine."

"This would be best," she quietly agreed.

"It's a damn shame," Bolan mused. "I may never pass this way again, and there's a lot of fruit to be picked down here."

"But, as you say, the tournament would now be a sham. They will be expecting you, and lying in wait for you."

"Yeah." Bolan sighed and dug into his moneybelt and produced a folded sheet of linen paper. He passed it over to the girl. "I took those names out of a book I came across in Las Vegas a couple of thousand years ago. They're the local reps—or they were, as of a day or so ago, of the mob's Caribbean operation, the entire wheel from Nassau to Panama."

Evita was scrutinizing the list of names in the fading light. "Yes, a few of these I recognize," she told him. "They make frequent visits at Glass Bay."

"Keep the list," he offered. "Give it to your bosses. Maybe it will tie in somewhere to their investigations. But tell them that they may as well cool it for a couple of months. I've an idea that those boys are all on sudden vacations. Or they will be, as soon as I'm officially declared free of the death trap here."

"There is one big name missing from this list," Evita said thoughtfully.

"Yeah? Which one?"

"You have heard the name Edward Stuart?"

Bolan smiled and shook his head. "If it's Mafia, and it's big, then it probably started as Eduardo Stuarti—but it still means nothing to me."

"This man is known as Sir Edward," Evita said casually. "He is thought to be the number one syndicate man in all of Caribe land. And this one would feel no need for a sudden vacation."

"That big?"

She nodded. "That big. He is thought to be very

118

influential behind the scenes in Haiti. Since Papa Doc's death, especially. I would—"

"Hold it," Bolan growled, his interest rising. "Are you saying this guy is in the Haitian government?"

"Officially, no. But, as I said, very influential. It is being said that the decline of tourism in Haiti during Papa Doc's regime is now being greatly reversed, and that Sir Edward Stuart is the man and the money behind this new surge."

"What is Puerto Rico's official interest in Stuart?"

"Officially, no interest," Evita replied. "Haiti is a free republic, a friendly neighbor. They belong to OAS and to the UN. But their government for many years has been a strong dictatorship, perhaps the most repressive and terroristic in the Americas. And Sir Edward's influence with certain officials provides him a perfect sanctuary from which to operate illegally throughout these islands. We are naturally interested, and we are naturally observing his operations whenever possible."

"Sanctuary, eh," Bolan commented.

"Yes. And you have heard of the syndicate money man who has taken sanctuary in Israel?"

Bolan nodded. "Who hasn't?"

"Well, couriers travel frequently between Tel Aviv and Port au Prince."

Bolan's eyebrows went up. "You aren't speaking of official government couriers."

"No."

Bolan said, "I see."

"My department fears a choking network of influence reaching from the Mediterranean to the Caribbean. And all centering about this untouchable Sir Edward Stuart."

119

"You're not suggesting that the Israeli and Haitian governments are cooking up—"

"Of course not. This is entirely a syndicate matter, not a political one."

"I have the feeling you're trying to sell me something, Evita," Bolan said soberly.

"But no, I am selling nothing. It is right that you should head for the home ground, as you say. Caribe will keep for another time."

She was wearing an entirely new hat now, Bolan decided.

He said, "Sure."

She said, "I speak, of course, from the greatest confidence. Sir Edward Stuart is the new Meyer Lansky of the western world. I thought you should know this. And that he enjoys the protection of the Haitian borders. He cannot be touched by any law, anywhere."

"Except one, eh?" Bolan replied, sighing.

She smiled and said, "Yes, except perhaps one."

"You're absolutely certain of the game?"

She soberly nodded her head. "The game is absolute."

Bolan fiddled with the safety of the Thompson. "Okay," he said gruffly. "I'll look in on Haiti on my way out."

She gazed into the palms of her hands and said, in the now familiar mimicry of Bolan's gruffness, "Okay. And good luck."

And Bolan knew that he'd been had by an expert.

He said, "You told me earlier that you had friends in high places. How high?"

She smiled and replied, "High enough."

High enough to set up an executioner. Sure. He

120

said, "There are no police lines at Puerta Vista, are there."

Very quietly she told him, "Not that one may notice. *I* am the police line, Mack Bolan."

He sighed and said, "I guess it's about time you proved that."

Smiling rather sadly, she opened her blouse and freed the sculpted breasts from the confining brassiere. She turned the cups out, parted the fabric liner, and removed a small scrap of vinyl material. Reproduced upon the vinyl was a miniaturized identification card, complete with photo and official embossment. Bolan sighed and gave it ack to her.

He watched her get herself back together, then he said, "Well, it's been a hell of a war game, hasn't it. You couldn't have set it up all the way, though. You've been playing it by ear, haven't you."

She said, "Yes. From the moment I realized that you were at Glass Bay. I spoke the truth, however, concerning the strike force. They are present, and they do strongly desire your body. I was ordered to do whatever possible to insure that you met death at Glass Bay. That failing, I was to attempt to contact you and lead you to San Juan, where you would be forcibly met. But then *you* contacted *me*, and in a most dramatic manner." She tapped her breast. "I also have certain discretions which I may employ as the occasion may demand. If this is what you say playing by ear . . ." She shrugged and looked away.

He told her, "You do a great bedroom scene, Big Eve. Another discretion?"

"I will admit that it began deliberately," she replied. "But it did not continue in that fashion. You must remember that."

Bolan would never forget. He smiled soberly and

"*Senor* Bolan!" he cried. "I feared you would not come!"

Bolan squeezed the boy's shoulders with both hands and said, "What's the panic, Juan? Couldn't you get the boat?"

"*Si*, I have the boat. But . . . ."

"But what?"

"They have my Rosalita!"

Bolan groaned, "Oh hell."

"They say they will feed her to the sharks! They say it is a trade, *you* for *her*."

Calmly, Evita said, "Tell us what happened, Juan."

The boy's eyes dropped and he replied, "I did not follow the instructions. Rosalita did not wish to go to my uncle's without me. She insisted upon remaining with me and waiting in the truck while I conduct the business." The agonized gaze lifted in a search of Bolan's impassive face. "I allowed her to do so. It is my fault, all of it."

"What do they want you to do, Juan?" Bolan asked him.

"They wish that I go on as though nothing is changed. I am simply to meet you and take you to the boat." The eyes fell again as he added, "They would not have learned these arrangements from me, *senor*, except that I am so fearful for Rosalita. These men are *muy malo*—very bad."

Bolan could have told the kid that the *muy malo* men would have learned, with or without Rosalita. The girl simply provided them the delightful free kicker, the insurance ticket.

Evita commented, "Why did they not simply spring the trap here? Why take the chance with Juan?"

123

She was not that familiar with the Mafia mind. Bolan was.

It was another example of super-care, super strategy for the super kill. When they could control a situation, they controlled it to the finest detail. The one thing they had not taken into account was Juan Escadrillo's monumental faith in Mack Bolan. The kid was placing the whole thing in Bolan's hands, confident that he would handle the situation to Rosalita's best advantage.

Bolan asked Juan, "How did they get onto us?"

"They are watching every one, every where. I did not know this, but they have enlisted spies from the men of the village."

Bolan nodded. "Okay, I should have known better. My goof, Juan, not yours, so stop hating yourself. I gave them too damn much time. All right, Juan, what's the plot?"

"The plot is this. I am to take you to the fisherman's wharf, at the center of town. This is the market place, and also the place where the sporting boats and the commercial fishers are kept. The boat I have hired for you has been moved to the end of the wharf. Next to this is the other boat, the one in which they hold my Rosalita."

Bolan was thinking of Monte Carlo and a very similar setup involving Tony Lavagni. The old triggerman was at least a consistent planner.

"This is a very powerful—what you call a cruiser, a sportfishing boat. We will have to walk directly past it in order to reach your boat."

"And they have Rosalita aboard the cruiser," Bolan commented.

"*Si.* They tell me to be very careful, and my Rosalita will not be harmed. Otherwise . . . ." The boy

124

shivered. ". . . . they will chop her into little pieces and use her for fishing bait."

"We won't let that happen," Bolan assured him.

"Rosalita sends this message. She says you should not think of her, nor of me, but that you should guard your own treasures, Mack Bolan."

Bolan's eyes were glinting crystals of ice.

He said, "That's exactly what I'm going to do, Juan."

11: BREAKOUT

Puerta Vista was located in one of the less scenic areas of the Caribbean coast. The shoreline was rocky, the natural harbor was small and shallow, and tourist accommodations in the tiny village were minimal and unpretentious. Puerta Vista was a fishing village, and most who lived there made their living from the sea.

The community wharf area reflected this state of existence. It was primarily a marketplace and the center of local activity. The wharf itself fronted the entire central district and provided mooring facilities for the local fishing fleet. A small area at the west end was reserved for "public" boats—the occasional non-commercial yacht or cruiser which might put into Puerta Vista for fuel or supplies.

To conserve docking space, the harbormaster had some years earlier instituted the "Mediterranean moor" as the docking method at Puerta Vista. This is a stern-to technique, with the boats backed into the dockage and secured by stern lines to the wharf, bow lines to buoys. Using this method, Puerta Vista had managed to accommodate her local commercial fleet while maintaining open wharfage for the growing numbers of pleasure boats which had lately begun making port calls.

The setup pleased Tony Lavagni immensely. The public dock space was well removed from the market area, and something like a hundred feet of open wharf separated his cruiser from the nearest fishing boat.

The old salvage rig which had been hired for Bolan's escape was tied up right next door, to the west of the cruiser, and these were the only two boats in the public dock.

A warehouse of corrugated sheet metal stood between this end of the wharf and the town. Bolan would have to walk along the entire western side of the wharf in order to reach his boat. He would also have to pass behind the cruiser. The only other way was through or over the warehouse, and Quick Tony had made provisions for that route also. As for swimming in—forget it. Quick Tony Lavagni was not born yesterday.

So he was ready, the taste of victory strong on his palate. Even if somehow Bolan should manage to get past them and onto his boat, he'd never make it out of the harbor. This "Med moor" bit was tailor-made for a fast getaway. The guy had told him that the U.S. Navy used the method for its Sixth Fleet operations in the Mediterranean, so they could haul out of port on a moment's notice, without all the dicking around with tugs and crap trying to get underway.

Bolan might like the setup too, naturally. As long as he didn't think there was any chance of a hot pursuit out of that place. The cruiser could run rings around that falling-apart salvage boat, so just let the hotshot bastard try some of his razzle-dazzle around here. He'd find out damn quick how far he could get with it.

Tony had six guns on the cruiser itself, and two of those were heavy automatics. He had two boys up on top of the warehouse with shotguns, and two more inside. He had boys spotted all along that wharf, mixing it up with the local yokels and ready to fall in behind Bolan and plug any escape out the back door. And he had a boy stationed on the salvage rig, just for the kicker. Bolan, Quick Tony was absolutely certain, would never set a foot on that boat.

It was a lot different here than at Monte Carlo. If it hadn't been for police interference, Lavagni would have nailed Bolan at Monte Carlo and ended all the anguish once and for all.

But there would be no such interference here. The village had one hick constable or something, sheriff maybe, a real comedian with a uniform like a Manhattan hotel doorman and about the same police ability.

Also, Tony had this time been given plenty of time to set the thing up properly. He had Bolan right where he wanted him, by the balls *that's where*, and Quick Tony could hardly wait to start squeezing.

Nothing could go wrong, nothing. Even if the kid suddenly lost his mind and tipped the thing to Bolan—even that wouldn't change anything.

Bolan fancied himself as a Sir Galahad or something when it came to the dames. He had even put his head on the block for a bunch of damn French whores—if the guy had a weak point, that was it. He couldn't walk away from a dame in trouble.

The pregnant kid broad meant nothing at all to Tony Lavagni. He didn't let himself get involved with people that way. She wasn't a *people* at all, she was just a *tool*, and he'd use her any damn way he could. He's shove a hook up her ass and dangle her from the yardarm if he thought that would bring Bolan around.

Bolan knew that, too.

And Bolan was a sucker for people.

The guy had a real people problem.

And he was going to lose his goddamn head over that problem. His first mistake was in sending that dumb hick kid in to do a man's job. Lavagni couldn't understand Bolan pulling a stunt like that, unless the guy was really getting desperate. Or unless . . . .

Quick Tony began to fidget. Maybe the bastard was just setting him up. Maybe he never intended to actually use that boat. Maybe he'd sent the kid in as a diversion, nothing more. Maybe he was suckering Tony into concentrating everything at Puerta Vista while he slipped out some other way.

Lavagni tried to dismiss the idea. Hell, he had to play the hand that was there, didn't he? Bolan was no god, he was no superman. Everybody made dumb mistakes now and then, even cagey shits like Mack Bolan. Still, Quick Tony couldn't help wondering about . . . .

He looked around and caught the eye of Joe Fini, crew chief on the cruiser. "Any word yet from Charlie?" he asked him.

Fini shook his head and replied in a near-whisper. "We been trying to raise him ever since we got docked. Maybe something's gone wrong with the radio. You want me to go down and try the car radio?"

Lavagni emphatically shook his head no. "Not now, hell. What about Latigo?"

"We ain't heard nothing from him for two hours, since he went west."

130

"I told Charlie to send all those boys to Puerta Vista."

"Well they was covering a lot of territory," Fini whispered. "I guess it takes awhile to get 'em all back together. This radio stuff ain't all it's cracked up to be."

"What the hell are you whispering about?"

Fini laughed self-consciously. "I guess it's just the mood around here. I feel like tip-toeing when I walk."

Lavagni growled, "Well tiptoe in there and see how our little madonna is making out. I don't want her losing her mind yet, I might need it."

"For what, Tony?"

"Never mind for what. Just cheer her up, make her feel like it's all gonna turn out okay. It ain't, of course, but you've been lying to broads all your life so go tell some more lies."

"Hell, I don't parleyvoo her lingo," Fini replied.

"Then use sign language. But watch where you put your hands. I don't want her going into shock right now."

Fini grinned wickedly and said, "Party pooper."

Lavagni shook his head disgustedly. "You call that a party? A pregnant cow?"

"They make the best lay," Fini told his boss. "They got everything to gain and nothin' to lose." He laughed and moved softly toward the cabin.

Lavagni watched him disappear inside, then he returned his attention to the wharf.

Hurry up Dammit, hurry up.

Lavagni lit a cigar and brooded over the situation for several minutes. Fini came back on deck and whispered, "She's okay. A little bit uptight, but

131

okay. I think she figures Prince Charming will come riding up any time now."

"I wisht he would," Quick Tony complained.

Fini chuckled and moved back to his station.

Lavagni craned his head about, spotting the other boys. Everybody was ready. *Every thing* was ready. Why didn't the bastard come on and get it over with? That kid told him eight o'clock, and here it was nearly eight thirty already.

It was almost as bad as the wait at Glass Bay. Lavagni shivered, remembering the awful scene they'd had there.

Well it wasn't going to happen here. It wasn't going to—

He stiffened and took a closer look along the wharf. Something was going on down there. The Manhattan doorman was moving around and people were taking off.

A chill trickled along Lavagni's spine. He turned around to whisper to Fini, "Get set, something's coming off."

Shops were closing, hastily, and the marketplace was being cleared. This was supposed to be the late-closing night. That guy had told Lavagni that those shops wouldn't close until nine o'clock. So what the hell was . . . ?

The rube cop was walking along the line of fishing boats now, yelling something in Spanish. Guys were jumping off onto the wharf and beating it.

Fini hoarsely called over, "What the hell is it, Tony?"

"I dunno," Lavagni shot back. "But if that big rube comes this far, you know what to do with 'im."

The cop spun around, though, and went back toward the middle. Evidently his only interest had been in clearing the commercial area. While Lavagni was pondering this, the cargo lights came on all along the wharf, brightly illuminating the entire strip.

A growl began deep in Lavagni's throat and he told Fini, "Okay, give the signal. The guy's coming, and I think maybe with help."

"You think he's got the law on his side, Tony?"

"Shut up what I think. Just give the signal."

Fini went to the flying bridge and briefly illuminated the big spot-light, then he returned tensely to his station. "Okay," he whispered.

"Cool it, now," Lavagni warned, in a voice loud enough to be heard in the immediate dock area. "Follow my lead."

And then a lone figure could be seen moving quickly along the wharf from the marketplace. The toonerville cop fell in beside him—and it was just the kid—and the two of them moved unhesitatingly along the line of fishing boats and into the public area.

Lavagni softly called out, "Watch it, now. It's going to be a razzle-dazzle, so look alive."

And then the kid and the toonerville comedian were standing there at the stern gangway. Lavagni was trying to look everywhere at once and wondering what the hell the guy was trying to pull when the kid's voice came across, taut but well under control.

"We have come for Rosalita."

"How do you want her?" Lavagni sneered back. "By the pound or by the pint?"

The toonerville cop got into it then. "It is illegal to hold a citizen of Puerto Rico against the will. If you

133

are holding a woman in this manner, you will surrender her at this once."

Quick Tony wanted to laugh out loud.

That fuckin' comic cop didn't even carry a gun.

He said, "Well I'll tell you what. We'll look around and see if we got a stowaway on board after we leave here. If we find one, and we just might, then we'll send her back C.O.D., in a shark's belly."

The kid stiffened and thrust his chin forward. "I bring a message for a *Senor* Quick Tony."

Lavagni's pulse leaped. The bastard knew who he was going against! Okay, great. That made it personal, and that made it all the sweeter. He called back, "So deliver the message."

"*Senor* Bolan accepts the challenge. He will fight you, in this place, at this time."

"So why ain't he here?" Lavagni sneered.

"He is here. He watches you at this very moment. But he will not fight while Rosalita is in the way of harm. You must release her first. Then he will fight."

Lavagni's eyes became busier. He shouted, "You gotta be kidding! I'm not falling for a routine like that!"

"My *senor* has said to tell you this. It is a Mexican stand-off. You will understand this meaning, he thinks. He says that you will not release Rosalita even if he gives himself up. He says that you will kill us all, that it is your way. Therefore, he feels that he will not be aiding Rosalita in this manner. But he desires to fight with Quick Tony. He desires this very much. Release the girl, he says, and he will bring to you the thunder and lightning you so richly deserve."

Fini croaked, "That's a crock of shit if I ever heard it!"

The big dumb rube cop was just standing there like a bump on a log, gazing about him like a tourist on a sightseeing trip. The kid was standing there in a fighting stance, legs spread defiantly, jaw thrust forward—mad as hell and telling it like it was, Lavagni had to figure.

"You will notice that the officer has cleared the area," the kid yelled. "It is at my *senor's* bidding. He is ready for the fight. He says to tell you this. When you have come from behind the woman's skirts, you will also be ready for the fight. Do you receive this meaning?"

"Don't fall for that shit, Tony!" Fini urged.

But Lavagni's mind was clicking through the situation. He called over, "What if I tell your *senor* to go to hell? What if I tell 'im we're going to have a gang bang on the poop deck with this little knocked-up girlie, and then we're gonna run what's left of her down the anchor chain for the sharks. How's he going to feel about that?"

"He has anticipated such a heinous action. He says, if this threat should be carried out, he will fade away into the night, Quick Tony, and he will take his own revenge in his own way, and at his own time. This is his message, it is all, it is final. If you desire a fight, then you know the conditions."

"Awright, just a second," Lavagni replied.

He called Fini over and said, "He's right, it's a Mexican stand off."

"Yeah but if you let the broad go, then you lose our only ace."

"It's not an ace anymore, that's just the point," Lavagni said. "It's a damn joker now. It's my fault, I messed up. I should've known, Bolan won't come

135

storming up here if he thinks the broad might get caught in his own fire."

"Do you know the guy that well, Tony?"

"I could write a book about the guy," Lavagni replied. "Also I never did figure the guy to just walk in and give hisself up. He's not that damn stupid."

"Well I guess we got only one play to make," Fini decided.

"That's the way I read it, Joe. We let the kid go and we take our chances on the 50-50 line. Either he'll come on in then or he won't. I think he will. It's like him. I think he'll make a play for the boat. He likes that wild razzle-dazzle stuff, and I guess he's getting tired of playing it cute. I'm betting the guy is ready for a showdown."

Fini sighed. "You're the boss," he said. "For the record, I'm with you. Personally, I don't like the way this uniformed dodo is acting up, this town constable. I'm afraid he knows something we don't. He might have a whole damn force hurrying down from San Juan or someplace, or maybe a vigilante group to back 'im up. Personally, Tony, I'm ready to either shit or get off the pot."

"Okay, go get the broad," Lavagni growled.

He turned back to the wharf and showed them his eyes and the top of his head and nothing else. "I'm calling your *senor's* bluff," he announced. "And you tell 'im he better have plenty of that thunder and lightnin' to spare, because I'm gonna shove it right up his ass."

"Be assured, it is no bluff," the kid replied.

And then Fini was there with the broad and shoving her toward the gangway. She saw the kid and let out a muffled little cry and he met her halfway and helped her to the wharf.

136

Another broad came running down from the market area—a real looker. She was barefooted and wore a grimy looking blouse and a short skirt, and Lavagni thought she looked vaguely familiar, but he could not place her in his immediate memory.

The two broads hugged each other, and they were crying and carrying on. The toonerville cop had walked on to the end of the dock and was just standing there with his arms folded across his chest and watching the tearful reunion in front of the cruiser.

The prick would probably take all the credit. He'd probably become a local legend, the big bad marshal without a gun who faced the fearful gangsters and took back the *senorita* from their clutches, a regular Wyatt Earp of Puerto Rico. Lavagni was thinking that the fuckin' comedian had better get the hell clear—that is, unless Bolan turned out to be a total damn four-flusher.

And then Tony had another inspiration. He flourished his revolver and leaned over the railing and sighted down on Juan Escadrillo. "Hey you, kid!" he snarled. "The girl goes but you stay"

"Senor?"

"Yeah, you, with the big mouth. You hired the fuckin' goddam boat, didn't you? Awright now, you go sit on the goddam thing!" He waggled the revolver menacingly. "Go on, get aboard the scow. And we'll see if your great *senor* can make it over there to join you."

The girl cried, "Juan, no!"

The other broad had some brains, though. She dragged the girl away, talking to her a mile a minute in Spanish, and the boy just stood there, and watched until they were well down the wharf, then

137

he flashed a smile toward the cruiser and called up, "With pleasure I go to await my *senor*."

Lavagni felt like plugging the wise-ass, but he let him cross over and jump aboard the salvage rig. Then Quick Tony threw back his head and shouted, "Okay Bolan! Let's hear some of that famous thunder of yours!"

The hick constable in the admiral's uniform was moving toward the protection of the salvage boat.

Not that way, dummy, Tony thought, you'd do a lot better in another direction. When Bolan comes, he'll come shooting and a'snorting. What the hell did this guy think he was, for crissakes, a goddam referee or something?

Come on, Bolan. Come on, baby, and let me taste your ass. Any way you want to show it. Try a line plunge in a car, that would be cute.

Come down the top of the warehouses—or try moving from boat to boat, like at Monte Carlo—only this time, baby, it's just you and me, Tony Lavagni and his quivering fate that's been playing hidey-seek all his life.

You, Bolan, *you* are Tony Lavagni's fate, his destiny. I owe you every fucking thing that I am right now, and I owe you everything that I'm going to become, a *Capo* you dumb shit, that's what you've made me. Well come on, come on. What the hell are you waiting for?

"Let's hear some thunder, Bolan!" he screamed.

From the corner of his eye he saw the big hick down on the wharf lighting a cigarette, and Tony thought what a hell of a thing to be doing at a time like this—was it some kind of signal? Then the guy was putting the pack of cigarettes back inside his coat, and his hand came out moving fast—oh hell

138

much too damn fast—and something long and bulky was flying toward the cruiser.

For one awful and timeless instant that thing hung there in the cargo light of the warehouse, suspended in Tony's vision and in the air above the cruiser, and in that final micro-second of understanding, Quick Tony recognized that thing for what it was. It was a bundle of dynamite sticks, tied together with a cluster of blasting caps.

And then time moved on, and the thunder descended, and the last impression to find registration in Lavagni's horrified eyes was that big dumb hick comic constable sprinting gracefully across the end of the wharf, a big black blaster filling one hand and spitting destruction into the roof of the warehouse.

It had been no more than a fifty-fifty chance, and Quick Tony had won his bet, the guy had shown up, he'd been there all the time, and Quick Tony had met his fate at last.

And as he was lifted into that weightless midst of thunder and lightning, Quick Tony knew that he could thank Mack Bolan for everything he would never become.

12: THE DEAL

The impact bomb had come in at dead center, instantly disintegrating the superstructure and lifting the entire cruiser out of the water. Her restraining lines were ruptured and the once-flashy speedster resettled at a crazy angle and drifted slowly into the channel, ablaze from stem to stern.

Nothing could have remained alive in that flaming wreckage. Bolan's attention had instantly swerved to the threats from other quarters, and the trusty Beretta had dispatched two gunners from the roof of the warehouse and another who had come running along the wharf.

And then he was aboard the old salvage boat and helping Juan cast off the stern lines. The ancient rig was made of stronger stuff than the Glass Bay cruiser. She had absorbed the blast shock with hardly a quiver and rode out the resultant minor tidal wave like a true queen of the seas.

Juan told Bolan, "The engine is turning. The moment I step aboard, I instruct the captain to make ready."

That was not all Juan had done the moment he stepped aboard. Sprawled out beneath the gangway was a guy in Glass Bay uniform, a gun in his clenched fist, the eyes wide and staring in surprise and fixed that way in death. Buried in his chest to the hilt was a heavy knife. The gun was a Beretta Brigadier, same model as Bolan's.

Bolan took the Beretta and shook several spare clips from the dead man's waistband, then he picked up the body and heaved it over the side.

There was a lot of running around and yelling farther up the pier, but no one seemed ready to venture down for a closer look.

The boat was heading into the channel. A guy with a big handlebar mustache and a very worried face thrust his head out of the cabin and yelled something aft in very rapid Spanish.

Juan looked up with a grimace and called back, *"Gracias, Capitan. Vamos ustedes, con todo velocidad!"*

He reported to Bolan, "He says the bow lines are clear and we are underway. I tell him to get the hell out of here."

Quickly, Bolan said, "Ask him if we can hook onto that pile of junk and haul it clear before the whole port is in flames."

Juan nodded and hurried forward.

Bolan remained aft to guard their rear, but no further hostile actions seemed impending—and soon he was assisting the three-man crew and Juan in the delicate business of grappling and towing a flaming marine disaster out to sea. They left the burning hulk wallowing in its own ashes a mile offshore.

They headed west then, Bolan instructing the skipper to remain within sight of shore. "Alert me immediately," he requested, "if any other vessels seem to be closing on us or crossing our course."

The captain signaled his understanding. Bolan and Juan went into the main cabin—a low-headroom affair with four bunks, a small galley, mess table, and various rough conveniences.

The mate came in behind them, grinning, to serve a half-and-half mixture of rum and hot coffee. Bolan tasted it and decided against it. He got out of the uniform which Evita had borrowed from the town constable and carefully folded it and placed it on a bunk.

The mate was very taken with the black combat suit. He grinned at Juan, murmured, *"Magnifico, magnifico"*—and went back on deck.

Juan stared into his cup and announced, "I killed a man, *Senor* Bolan."

How many had Bolan killed?

He said, "Yeah, I noticed," and spread out a map which Evita had given him during those tense moments at Puerta Vista. He sat at the table with the map, gave Juan a close scrutiny, then added, "A man has a right to protect his treasures. No, he has an obligation."

"If I had your skills, *senor*," Juan replied quietly, "I would kill them all. They are scum, filth—they are wild beasts with no humanity in them."

"That's what I keep telling myself," Bolan muttered.

"My Rosalita. You think she is safe now?"

"She's entirely safe, Juan. Don't worry, she's in good hands."

"She told me, before, at the first, that you would come. But she also hoped that you would not. She was fearful for you, *senor*."

Bolan said, "How're you feeling?"

"Fine. I am feeling like a man. I envy you, *senor*."

"Don't," Bolan growled. "You have life where it's all at, *amigo*. Place of your own, a decent life, a

143

good woman to share it with, a kid coming to give it all meaning. What is there left to envy?"

"You are right."

Bolan fell to studying the map. He shoved it toward Juan and tapped a spot with his finger. "Tell the captain to put me in there at precisely midnight."

The boy finished his rum-coffee and moved toward the door.

Bolan said, "Juan . . . I'm damn proud of you."

This drew a flashing smile. "You rest," Juan told him. "I will take the watch on deck until midnight."

"Thanks. To tell the truth, I'm about out of my head. I can't remember the last time I slept."

"Sleep now, *Senor Magnifico*. I have never myself felt more awake in all of my life."

The kid went out, and Bolan tumbled onto a bunk.

Yeah.

Sleep now.

Kill later.

It was not over yet.

Jack Grimaldi eased the company car into Glass Bay and pulled up behind the office. The blackened hulk of the main house stood grimly deserted but both bungalows were blazing with light and some sort of noise contest seemed to be going on between the two. The boys had come back with booze and women, and quite a party was underway. The amplified throbbing of recorded rock was blasting from both camps above the hubbub of male voices and the gay shrieks of hired women.

As Grimaldi stepped out of the car a nude cutey burst from a doorway above the carport and ran

144

laughing down the stairs with a guy in jockey shorts chasing close behind. They ran past him without a glance, headed toward the beach.

It was a celebration. A wake for Bolan, Grimaldi guessed.

He avoided the bungalows and went to the grassy area behind the carports. Air Two sat there gleaming in the moonlight, deserted and forlorn with her work all done. The pilot from San Juan was no doubt partying it up with the hardmen, celebrating a death which all Mafiadom had been working toward.

Grimaldi slid inside and checked the fuel situation.

It was terrible.

He returned to the carport and found a five-gallon can, took it to the gas pump, and began the laborious process of refueling the 'copter.

Grimaldi did not feel like partying.

Nor did he feel like hanging around Glass Bay any longer than was absolutely necessary.

It was a thirty minute job of pumping, lugging, and filling—over and over again—and the party had lost no steam at all during that period.

He made an extra trip, for future contingencies, and secured the five-gallon spare inside the cabin of the helicopter.

Grimaldi was getting the hell out of Puerto Rico, as fast as those rotors would carry him.

It had been a hell of a day, though, and he needed one final item for the road. He entered the end bungalow through the kitchen door, shoved a clinched half-nude couple out of the way, and snared a bottle of bourbon from the open case on the table.

The guy was a total stranger and the girl was drunk. She mumbled something like "*Por favor*," and Grimaldi muttered, "Yeah, same to you," and went back outside.

The moon was high and Glass Bay was basking in its soft radiance. A paradise, sure. Under somewhat different circumstances, Grimaldi could have really enjoyed the joint. But those sheet-wrapped bodies were still laid out over there. By morning they would be stinking. He shivered and went the other way. Couldn't they at least dump their dead before the orgy?

He went on around to the front and gazed out across the bay as he opened the bottle. *Bahia de Vidria*, the bay of glass. Yeah, broken glass, shattered, and nobody would ever put the pieces back together again. Not for Jack Grimaldi, that was for sure.

He heard a boat chugging along somewhere in the distance, and he wondered how ordinary people made the pieces of their lives fit, how they used their mundane lives, how they bridged the awful gulfs between hope and despair, dreams and disillusionment, challenge and failure.

Jack Grimaldi's life had been failing steadily since birth.

Life itself was one big *schtick*.

But Grimaldi was not yet quite ready to write it all off. He had not even reached the midpoint yet ... he hoped. In a few more months he'd be thirty. Maybe. Twice this day he had stared into death, and twice he had walked away from that unsettling view. It was enough to make a guy think.

He took a deep pull from the bottle, choked,

wiped the spillage away, and looked at his watch. Ten minutes past midnight.

Yeah, it had been a hell of a day.

He stared back around the burned-out hulk and walked straight into the big mean bastard in the black suit.

He was wearing one of those tight, mirthless smiles, and he said, "Enjoying the party, Jack?"

Goodbye, thirtieth birthday. So the son of a bitch had made it through, after all.

Grimaldi sighed and said, "Okay, where do you want to go this time?"

The guy chuckled—like a skeleton clearing its throat. "You got some wings?"

"Sure." He uncorked the bottle and handed it over. "The windmill type. Gassed up and ready to fart. What the hell are you doing here, Bolan?"

The guy refused the bottle. "Looking for wings," he said. The bastard didn't waste many words. "And a pilot."

"You don't want to hang around and crash your own party?"

"That's my party?"

"Sure. I guess I never got around to correcting an erroneous impression. But let's not tell them now," he added hastily. "I figure let 'em live a little. You know? Or no, I guess you wouldn't know. I, uh, I caught your fireworks at Puerta Vista."

The guy had him by the arm and they were walking quietly toward the rear, skirting close beside the end bungalow. He said, "Yeah?"

"Yeah. But I, uh ... I guess I jumped to a hasty conclusion. Well, I guess the curtain was for Lavagni, huh?"

"Buried at sea," the guy said.

147

"Uh huh. It figures better that way. Uh, after you turned me loose I circled back along the waterfront. Sat there on a damn rock just outside of town, and I guess I was thinking about a lot of things. Then I heard the ba-loom and I saw the flames, and I said, 'Contact, there goes Bolan.' I guess I should have said, 'Ho ho, there's Bolan!' Well anyway, I sat there a little while longer, then I went on into town and found one of the company cars. I hotwired the ignition . . . and here I am with a lonely bottle at a false wake."

He didn't know why he told the guy all that. He wasn't talking for his life, and this realization came with quite a shock. He didn't give a damn anymore; that was the shocking part. He just didn't give a damn.

They reached the helicopter and they stood there for a moment, the big guy just sort of looking around, then those icy eyes lit on Grimaldi and he said, "I've noticed you don't pack hardware, Jack."

"Never," the pilot replied unemotionally. "My only crime, Bolan, is carting these clowns around. It brings me two grand a month and an unlimited credit card for expenses. The price of a soul, eh? But it beats anything else that turned up after . . ."

"After what?" the guy asked, as though he was really interested.

"Well . . . you don't know the routine. I mean, you never really tried the returning serviceman routine. You just went from one war right into another. No employment problems, right?"

"You were at 'Nam?"

"Yeah. Flew everything from single-engine scouts to Huey close supports. Enlisted pilot, later a warrant officer. You know what kind of jobs I got offered when I got home?"

Bolan said, "I can guess."

"Well, a cousin got me this job. And I kissed his shoes for it. But I guess ..."

"You guess what?"

"Nothing. Where're you hijacking me to this time?"

A soft hardman staggered across the yard about twenty feet from where they were standing and disappeared around the carport.

The big guy watched him out of sight, then he dug inside his suit and fumbled around with something at his waist and came out with a lot of green. He counted the stuff out, twelve Clevelands, and laid it in Grimaldi's palm.

"No hijack this time," he said gruffly. "I came looking for you specifically, Jack. I want to take you up on that suggestion that we laughed about earlier. I'd like to pay your salary for a day. That's what's left of my warchest, twelve thou."

Yeah, the guy was too much. Grimaldi mumbled, "What th' hell, all you gotta do is point the gun, I'll fly you anywhere."

"Special mission," the guy said.

"Yeah?"

"Yeah. Not the kind you take a guy into with a gun at his head. I need you. Your skill and your guts. I mean, cooperatively. What do you say?"

The fuckin' guy was insane!

"Do I have to handle a gun?"

"Not unless you want to."

"This a kill mission, Bolan?"

"Yeah."

"A biggee?"

149

"A hell of a biggee."

"Suppose I say no?"

The guy shrugged. "Then the hit is off, I hijack you back to the mainland, we go our separate ways."

"A real biggee."

"A hell of a biggee."

So what the hell. It was the end of *schtick*.

Grimaldi counted off six of the Clevelands and gave them back to Mr. Death. "Split it down the middle," he said quietly. "And call it a deal."

13: DEATH BRIEF

An old salvage boat cruised a slow circle in the sparkling Caribbean several miles off *Bahia de Vidria*. In the pilot house, Juan Escadrillo stood a tense watch over the radio equipment while the man with the handlebar mustache stared expectantly into the moonlit skies.

The mate brought coffee from the galley, and drank most of it himself, and twice the engineer came topside to restlessly roam the deck and gaze toward shore, and the quiet watch went on.

At almost exactly 12:30 the radio in the pilot house crackled and a familiar voice came through the international distress frequency to give the awaited announcement.

"Okay Juan, we're off and running. The number here is 25, 12, 12, 14. That is two-five, one-two, one-two, one-four. Thanks to all of you. And give those treasures back there my, uh, deepest regards."

"A-OK," Juan replied immediately. "Run with luck, my friend."

"*Adios, amigo.*"

"Return to us one day."

"I'll try, Juan. Leave a light in the window."

"It will be there."

The boy's eyes were brimming with moisture as

151

he shifted the gear to the harbor frequency. The crew had moved outside to search the sky for visible evidence of the small aircraft.

Juan made the call in the Spanish language. "This is salvage tug Salvadore calling Puerta Vista Harbormaster."

"Go ahead, Salvadore."

"I am ready with the Matilda report."

Evita Aguilar's voice responded. "Matilda. Go ahead, Salvadore."

"It is done. A-OK. The numbers are two-five, one-two, one-two, one-four. He sends love. We return to port."

In the little shack on the Puerta Vista wharf, Evita turned away from the radio and spoke into a waiting telephone connection to San Juan.

"Success," she reported, using the official language. "It is clear. Suggest that you move on Glass Bay immediately."

"Right," was the reply. "We are moving."

"Connect me now with Glenn Robertson."

"Right, standby."

A moment later an American voice came on the line and the language shifted to English. "Robertson here."

"Glenn, Matilda."

"Save it, I know. Bolan busted loose."

"Yes. Ramirez is now moving on Glass Bay."

"Yeah, I heard. So there goes your sweet little intelligence drop. Should've played it my way, pretty lady."

"The sweet drop was gone the moment he arrived. Do not fear, we are awaiting the reorganization and we know whom to watch. As for

152

doing it your way, I would have more compassion on a pig in a slaughter pen."

The American sighed heavily. She heard the snap of a cigarette lighter and he said, "You know that none of us like the order, Matilda."

"We may as well drop the 'Matilda' now, also."

"Right, right. How come it's so hard to hate the guy, Evita? What's he got that John Dillinger and Pretty Boy Floyd never had."

"Integrity, maybe," she replied coldly.

"Well, that's a lot of deadly integrity you turned loose on the world, pretty lady."

"It is simply a matter of time, anyway," she told him. "The way this *hombre* operates, he cannot be long for this world."

"How many did he clobber there?"

"We will be counting the dead for days," Evita said. "Some may never be found."

"Well, that's Bolan. He leaves a hell of a wake. One of these days, Evita, the guy is *really* going to run amuck. He's going to start killing cops and little kids and anything that gets in his way. And then you'll understand why we—"

"That is a stupid idea!" Evita stormed. "This is as gentle and fine a man as I have ever known! *Policia estupido! Acerca de—*"

"Hold it, hold it, don't start throwing hot Spanish at me." The federal agent chuckled drily and added, "Sounds as though he made more than one kind of kill. Just how well did you get to know this fine gentle man, pretty lady?"

She said, "Get to hell, Glenn Robertson."

He said, "Well . . . I guess I better alert Washington. Battle stations, repel all boarders, and so forth.

Give me a clue, just a sniff. Where should we concentrate the defenses?"

"Never mind," she replied.

"What?"

"Never mind." Her voice broke as she added, "I have sent him to his death."

Grimaldi set the little bird down on the tiny island which gave its name to the Mona Passage, between Puerto Rico and Hispaniola, and the two-man assault team laid their battle plans and awaited the countdown to the kill.

Bolan studied terrain maps while the pilot pored over radio navigation charts and reviewed in his memory the various details of Haiti's border security setup.

"How long since you flew in there?" Bolan asked him.

"About three months ago," Grimaldi muttered. "Uh . . . put an X on your chart, uh . . . down here at Charlie Eight. There's a Haitian Coast Guard station there. They have radar and hot-pursuit capability. Also up at, uh, Bravo Three, a base for jet fighters."

"How good are they?"

"Can't say. Never had to evade them. Always had the right words."

Bolan studied his companion for a thoughtful moment, then he suggested, "Let's figure the withdrawal through the gap, on a 340 magnetic from Port au Prince. That looks like high mountains to the north."

"It is, and rugged as hell," Grimaldi replied. "They still have insurgents operating in those mountains."

"Perfect. If we have to take to the ground then

there'll be good cover and maybe even a helping hand along the way."

"Don't count on it," Grimaldi warned. "Most of the rebels have turned commie. They worship Che and Fidel, and I'll have to say that's a better alternative than Papa Doc. But America has become a nasty word in those hills, I hear."

"I thought the old man died," Bolan said.

"Yeah, but Doc Junior stepped right in, same regime, same ruthless repression. Look, Bolan, are you sure you know what you're getting into? That country is crawling with secret police. If they catch you, the nicest thing they can do for you is to show you the firing squad. They've got people chained in rat holes who haven't seen the light of day—or a courtroom, I might add—for more than ten years."

"Nice country," Bolan muttered.

"It's not the country, it's the government. They're blacks, you know. A bit of French mixed in here and there, but it's mostly black. And if the people at home think the panthers are mean, they need to clue in on this Haitian gestapo. They make the Mafia seem like gentleman students pranking around."

"Is Sir Edward black?"

Grimaldi's eyelids fluttered. "I couldn't say," he replied.

"You've never seen him?"

"No."

"How many times have you been into Sir Edward's joint?"

"Just once, my last trip in, three months ago."

"What was the occasion?"

"Meeting of the board. Finance matters."

"Who'd you bring in?"

"Manny Walters and his legal eagles."

"Manny the Muck?"

"The same."

"What's Detroit got going down here?"

"Bit of juice, I hear, among other things."

"You don't mean nickel and dime juice."

"Hell no, big league stuff. Unofficial loans for off-the-record business enterprises. And the take is high. I hear as much as thirty percent in some cases."

"The Haitian government condones that?"

Grimaldi shrugged. "What the hell is the government? In a country like this one, especially. Look, Bolan. Get the picture. The black people in our country have been screaming about white repression of blacks and all that jazz—and I'm not saying they shouldn't. They're right. Every guy has a right to his own shot at life, his own way. That's not the point. Here's a country that's all black. But it's not very beautiful down here. It's misery and poverty and repression like no American black man has experienced in this century. And he's getting it from his own brothers, see. I mean, when you speak of the Haitian government, you're talking about a gang of thieves and cutthroats with licenses."

"Okay, I have that picture," Bolan said.

"They're all on the take."

"Is Sir Edward a black man?"

"I told you I didn't know, dammit."

"What's his real name?"

"I don't know. In Haiti, he's Sir Edward Stuart. That's all I know."

"But he is not a citizen of Haiti."

"No, hell no. Look, Port au Prince is just the center. Everything down here revolves around that center."

"Who does Sir Edward belong to?" Bolan asked quietly.

Grimaldi snorted and replied, "It's the other way around, friend. Look, he's bigger than—look, get the picture straight, huh? Sir Edward Stuart is not a *Mafioso*."

"I understood that."

"A private pilot is like a bodyguard, you know. We hear all kind of stuff—but we're supposed to pretend that our ears are missing. This Sir Edward is an international biggee. I thought you knew that."

"I do. Who else is getting burned—other than the people of Haiti."

Grimaldi sighed. "Everybody, man. Cuba, even, and that's a whole ball game of its own. Fidel thinks he's got Cuba snockered. The poor sap. I could tell Fidel, capitalism is flourishing in his living room. And it's black money, and it's moving through Cuba like Ex-Lax."

"Panama bankers?"

The pilot nodded. "Same laws as Switzerland, you know. Hell, it's tailor-made for the Caribbean take-over."

"Then it really is a take-over," Bolan mused.

"You'd better know it is. Did you ever notice the way the good money always flows behind the blood money? Watch the so-called legit businessmen swarming toward the good thing. They know."

"What do you know about the Mediterranean tie-in?"

"What the hell is this, Bolan?" Grimaldi asked irritably. "A pump job or a hit?"

"It all figures in, Jack. The more I know, the better I can operate. What's this stuff about the Med?"

157

The pilot sighed and replied, "Just talk, that's all I know. A word here and there, a joke, a slip, it doesn't amount to much."

"Give."

"They just call it 'the island.' Somewhere in the Med, I don't know where. Someplace around Italy, I think—or maybe it's Greece. Hell, I don't know. The international *Commissione* meets there, I hear. It's like a little UN. But it's more than Mafia, bigger than Cosa Nostra. I don't know just how it's structured. But it's a cartel, Bolan. The world monopoly on organized crime. And it's big, daddy, it's damn big."

"And Tel Aviv?"

Grimaldi smiled sourly and said, "Shit you do have big ears. That guy is officially retired, I hear. He requested and received political sanctuary under the Israeli charter. You know, the inviolate home of the international jew. The Israeli government doesn't like it, I hear . . . I mean, giving refuge to a guy like him . . . but they're stuck with it, gored by their own constitution."

"*Is* he retired?"

"*That* guy?" Grimaldi snickered. "Does a shark turn into a goldfish in its old age?"

Bolan muttered, "It just goes on and on, doesn't it."

"Make you feel like you're trying to dam the tide with turds?"

Bolan growled, "Sometimes, yeah. But then I remember."

"You remember what?"

"I'm not here to cure, just to kill."

Grimaldi shook away a shiver and said, "Well, you

158

do that pretty well. And Sir Edward is next on tap. Right?"

"Right. You get me in there, Jack. That's all I ask."

"You don't want me to get you out?"

Bolan grinned. "I'd consider that a bonus. But yeah. Yeah, I'd like to get back out, Jack."

"That's my specialty. But tell me, Bolan. Why?"

"Why what?"

"Why this kill? Why any of them? What the hell are you winning? I mean, realistically now. You know the score. You pop one, he falls over, another steps up, you pop him, up comes the next guy. They're too big for you, fella. You're fighting a machine that fixes its own hurts. So why?"

"Crime pays," Bolan replied quietly. "It pays damn big."

"So what else is new? Was that supposed to answer my question?"

"Yeah. I'm not fighting a machine. I'm fighting people. People who intend to profit from crime. I'm showing some of them that there is no profit. Okay?"

Grimaldi said, "Okay. Maybe you're right. If you can stay alive and keep it going, then maybe so. Maybe you'll make it too damn hazardous for the next guy to step to the head of the line. But I doubt that you'll live that long, Bolan."

"I'm going to try."

"By trying a hit on the hell hole of the Caribbean? You keep trying that hard, buddy, and . . . aw, what the hell. Let's go do it."

"You got everything straight in your mind?"

Grimaldi glanced at his watch. "We have plenty

of time, let's run through that floor plan once more, just in case I forgot something."

Bolan shuffled the map to one side and laid out the diagram of the cliffside mansion near Port au Prince, as reproduced from Jack Grimaldi's memory of a brief visit three months earlier.

"Okay," he said. "North wall here, gate to the west, guard shack over here. Bedrooms—"

"Hell I'm glad I looked again," Grimaldi interrupted. "There's a courtyard between the east and west wings."

"Right here?"

"Yeah. Flower gardens and stuff. Uh, I think—yeah, French doors into the house, ground level. Security station down here at the corner."

"Hardmen?"

"Hard *black* men. Civilian clothes."

"Weapons?"

"Sidearms, concealed."

"How many at that station?"

"Two, I believe. Yeah, two."

"Okay, let's take the whole thing again, detail by detail. First floor, reception hall—a man and a dog. Right?"

"Right."

"Winding stairway up to the left, library to the right, ballroom straight ahead."

"Yeh, but they don't ball there."

"Kitchen, dining room, butler's pantry, security cell. Right?"

"Right. The cell is manned day and night. Electronically locked."

"Any idea about the duty shifts in that cell?"

"I think three. I saw them changing at midnight."

"Okay. Now. The guy in the cell. He monitors all three floors."

"Right. The television cameras are all over the place. They might even have hidden ones in the bedrooms. I wouldn't put it past them."

"Anything else about that first floor? Anything at all?"

Grimaldi pondered for a moment, then replied, "That's all I can draw."

"Okay, upstairs. Sir Edward's suite."

"I never got in there."

"Think of it from the outside."

"Well ... yeah, I told you ... uh, come to think of it, he must take the whole damn corner there. Let's see, the doors are ..."

"Think about it."

"I'm thinking. The guard in the hall and one in the inner security room. Let's see ... oh, all the inside guards are hard Mafia, I mean wops like me. Uh, I'll bet he has about three large rooms in that suite. I mean, not counting the security jazz."

"Women?"

"I never saw one on the whole place."

"Okay. Over to the west wing, now. Offices, conference rooms, a vault."

"Yeah."

"Second floor. Is this all the windows there are on the second floor west?"

"Hell I didn't build the damn place, I just spent an evening there."

"If you think hard enough, Jack, you could tell me all about your mother's womb. Are you saying there are just two damn windows on that whole floor?"

"Well now wait, no—I've got the stairs in the

wrong place. Look. Gimme the damn pencil. Here's the way...."

And so it went, toward the dawn.

The Caribbean Kill was definitely not over.

The big one was yet to come.

14: WITH THE DAWN

The Republic of Haiti is slightly larger than the state of Maryland and has a population estimated at close to five million people. Discovered by Columbus in 1492, it became a French colony in 1677, achieved independence from France in 1804, and has been a constituted republic since 1820. The ore-rich and agriculturally productive country has had a turbulent history, especially during the 20th century. Following a five year period of political tumult and violence, U.S. forces occupied Haiti in 1915 to restore order, this occupation lasting until the mid-1930's.

A surface calm prevailed over this troubled land until 1950, and then five successive governments rose and fell until the election in 1957 of "Papa Doc" Duvalier. That administration undertook a program of severe political repression and engineered a constitutional "reform" in 1964 which established Papa Doc as President of Haiti for life. The Duvalier years were marked by official terrorism, internal strife and rebellion, and open hostility between Haiti and her island neighbor, the Dominican Republic.

Through all of this tense history, the plight of the ordinary Haitian citizen seems to have shown little improvement. Illiteracy in the republic is common, wretched poverty a way of life.

It was not difficult for Mack Bolan to understand why Haiti had been selected as the hub of the Caribbean Carousel. A government which showed no official respect for its people would certainly be amenable to the influences of an "international invisible government" trafficking in the same brand of human exploitation and organized greed. They made a pair, Bolan decided—and he had to wonder how many other small and vulnerable countries around the world were being setup for invisible domination by the international cartel of crime.

The situation seemed a bit ironic. The giant "world powers" had been locking horns and cold-warring for international influence for most of three decades. They'd rattled rockets at one another, maintained huge armies, raced into outer space, fought or backed brushfire wars, and tried to woo the world with dollars, rubles, and yuans.

And quietly, through it all, the street-corner hoods of all the lands had been nickle-and-diming their way toward the formation of that brooding and overlying conglomeration which could certainly be called *The Fourth Power*. Without armies or foreign aid or space programs, they had invisibly welded themselves onto the throats of their societies and interlocked their tentacles in a whole new and devastatingly effective political idea—the new politics—the politics of rape and robbery—and they were making it work.

A guy didn't have to grow up in a ghetto to develop a criminal mentality. The neighborhood punks could never have brought it off without the assistance of that other criminal type—the businessman without a conscience, the politico without a soul, the lawyer with nothing but contempt for human justice.

There were some strange bedfellows beneath that Fourth Power sheet. There were, it seemed, entire government administrations, corporations, international financiers, "nice" people of every race and religion and political philosophy, hoods, punks, thugs, psychopaths—yeah, it was the little United Nations, all right. An entire fourth society brought together under one common banner: greed.

And they were eating the world.

Bolan was aware that his war was expanding. The battle fronts were extending in all directions at once, and into infinity.

What the hell could one man do in the face of all that?

Bolan knew that his was an extreme case of reaction. He could not expect others to follow his example, to abandon their own quests for happiness and fulfillment in exchange for unrelenting and unlimited warfare. But he could expect no less of himself.

He had been taught to kill. It was his trade, his profession. And he was good at it. He had the tools, the skills, and an awareness of the enemy. He could do no less than all-out war.

So what could one man do?

He could kill. He could cover himself with blood and offer up his own for the taking. He could stand up to the appetites of that voracious Fourth Power and shake his fist in their bloated faces. He could stay alive as long as possible while continuing the opposition. He could remind them that not every man had a price—that principle and dedication and audacity and guts were still alive in the human race.

165

He could remind them that there was a higher reason and purpose behind the forward spiral of human evolution, and that the universe would be kind to those who continued to reach beyond themselves toward the higher goals. He could dog them every step of the way, and hold up a mirror to their gross distortions of the estate of mankind, and show them that they were, *by God*, not going to get away with it.

And it was this overlying rationale that sent Mack Bolan into a foreign republic, with stealth and in darkness, to kill a man whom he had never heard of until a few hours earlier.

Jack Grimaldi's reasons were perhaps a bit more personally defined. He quit simply admired Mack Bolan, and he was thoroughly disgusted with the unadmirable course his own life had taken.

As they scuttled across the Haitian landfall in the helicopter, Grimaldi told Bolan, "When my cousin came to me with this proposition, I figured what the hell. I had the Italian name, I may as well live in the image."

"What image?" Bolan asked, though he knew.

"What the hell, if you're Italian you've gotta be Mafia. Right?"

Bolan grinned and replied, "Yeah I know, Jack. I grew up with Italians. I know them, as a people. It's a shame that a speck of dirt is able to tarnish the whole image."

"You like wops?" the pilot asked, smiling.

"Sure." Bolan patted his belly. "My stomach even remembers. It knew every kitchen in the neighborhood."

Grimaldi chuckled. "You got your strength from *pasta*."

Bolan replied, "Yeah, I—" then fell silent when his companion tensed suddenly and craned his head into a scan of the higher altitudes. "What is it?"

"The fuzz, I fear."

The earphones crackled then from an outside carrier wave and a breathless foreign voice delivered an officious announcement.

"You understand that?" Bolan asked the pilot.

"It's French Creole, no. But I know what he wants." Grimaldi touched the throat mike and announced, "*Helicoptere Americain, voyageur permettre* Port au Prince, Sir Edward *numero cinquante et un.*"

A propellor-driven military fighter plane buzzed them, flashing past in the darkness as a well-enunciated reply came in English.

"Welcome to Haiti." He pronounced it high-tie. "Please conform to established flight paths."

"Roger. Thanks."

Bolan showed his companion a tense grin and commented, "Real class."

"Oh they're classy as hell," Grimaldi told him. "Until they decide they don't like you."

"What was that number you gave him?"

"It's the one I was given to use last time. I don't know, maybe it's a standard code. Anyway, it worked."

"Anyone visiting Sir Edward can come and go without worrying about customs inspections?"

"That's the idea. I told you, man. He's a hand in their glove."

"I wonder what happens to the glove," Bolan mused, "when I chop off the hand."

"A glove without a hand isn't worth much," Gri-

167

maldi replied. "It'll find itself another one. That's what I meant. This war of yours is hopeless, man."

"Not until I'm dead," Bolan growled.

"You're already dead," Grimaldi said.

"Just sit there," Bolan told his newest ally, "and watch the dead walk again."

It was, after all, the land of the zombie.

The land of the living dead.

And Mack Bolan felt entirely at home.

The helicopter circled in a high, wide pass at "the mansion in the rocks" while Bolan studied the situation through binoculars. Lights were showing from every visible window, and a considerable number of cars could be seen in the vehicle area. Few other details were available, from this viewpoint.

"What's with this 'attack at dawn' jazz?" Grimaldi groused. "Is it just a tradition? They were always calling us out for dawn strikes in 'Nam, and I never could figure it out. Why dawn?"

Bolan continued the binocular surveillance as he replied, "Not entirely tradition. There's a psychological moment involved—also a biological one."

"Oh well, that answers my question entirely," the pilot said sarcastically.

"The human animal is a product of the planet," Bolan explained as he continued the scouting. "We've developed certain rhythms, both physically and mentally. Dawn is a sort of neutral area. For the guy that's been up all night, it means an inner letdown, a torpor."

"Really?"

"Yeah. In the jungle sense, it means a relaxation from the perils of the night—that is, for us daylight creatures. That hint of light in the sky means that

168

we've made it through another night, and we can relax now."

"So you relax and attack," Grimaldi commented. "Sounds brilliant."

"No," Bolan said. "You attack the guy who's fallen into a false sense of security."

"You won't find any false security down there, buddy."

"We'll see," Bolan said. "Put her down."

"You really going to trust me to come back and get you?"

"Yep."

The pilot grinned. "Think you're a pretty good judge of flesh, don't you?"

"Have to be," Bolan clipped back. "Put me down."

Grimaldi put him down, hovering just off the coastal rocks less than a hundred yards outside the high walls of the estate.

Bolan opened the hatch, said, "Good luck," and slid to the ground, a drop of about five feet.

Grimaldi leaned over to secure the hatch, murmured, "Yeah, good luck, what's that?"—and sent the little bird into a heeling climb toward the sea.

Bolan watched him disappear into the dusky overhead, then he took a sighting on his goal, checked his weapons, and moved silently toward the wall.

He was in blacksuit, face and hands also darkened, a gliding shadow in a landscape of darkness.

The moon was gone, and the first faint streaks of morning grayness were edging into the eastern horizon.

The timing had been perfect. So far. It had to be. Ten minutes . . . that was all the time he had.

He scaled the wall and dropped lightly inside the

grounds and moved swiftly on without pause, relying now entirely upon Jack Grimaldi's memories of things that had been—three months earlier.

Halfway across the compound Bolan was suddenly hit with the realization that things were almost *precisely* as they had been on that earlier occasion of Grimaldi's visit.

The damn joint was overflowing with people.

Visiting type people.

A large-scale meeting of the mob was evidently in progress, and had apparently been going on all night.

Bolan did not know it yet, but the Caribbean Conclave was in session. He would soon recognize a familiar face or two, and he would wonder if he had dropped into an executioner's heaven . . . or into hell itself.

And he had less than ten minutes to discover which it was to be.

The dawn was on the march.

And so was Death.

15: THE BIGGEE

The layout almost perfectly coincided with Grimaldi's diagram. Bolan quickly located the telephone cable and took away their communications with the outside world. He then went directly to the security station at the east side of the courtyard.

It was an elaborate little structure made of choice Haitian wood and polished to a dark lustre, about the size of a large American outhouse but with standing room only inside.

A row of closed circuit television monitors were banked along one wall, providing various exterior views of the grounds—including the wall Bolan had just come over.

An athletically built black man wearing a tight-fitting white suit was standing in front of the monitors, his back to Bolan, yawning and stretching and scratching the back of his head.

The Beretta phutted a quiet Parabellum in to help relieve the itch. It scrunched in between the clawing fingers and the guy pitched forward against the monitors and slid into a squat beneath them.

Another sentry came strolling in from a flower bed a few yards away, fiddling with the fly of his trousers. Yeah, even overloaded bladders wanted to let go at dawn. Bolan let go another zap from the

171

Beretta. The guy's head snapped back and he returned to where he'd been, lying in it now and not even knowing it.

Bolan grabbed the first guy by an ankle and dragged him into the flower bed and left him beside the other one.

He'd been a minute and a half inside the grounds. And not a peep from anywhere.

No false security, eh?

Next on the agenda was the guard shack at the other side. Bolan crossed over on a soft run, avoiding the lighted areas near the house, and found the shack attended by a single guard who was in the act of pouring coffee from a thermos into a plastic cup.

He waited until the guy set the thermos down, then he reached inside with both hands and lifted the sentry out, one big hand over the mouth and a forearm clamped into his throat.

One violent twist and the guy stopped struggling and went limp. Continuing the initial motion without breaking stride, Bolan carried him on to an automobile in the parking area and tucked the body inside.

A door opened several carlengths away, another white suite rose into hazy view, and a soft voice called out, "Henri?"

Bolan stood there behind the open car door and waited for the guy to come forward.

The prey came down hesitantly, halted at the front bumper, and again said, "Henri?"

He was a large one. Apparently he'd been goofing off in one of the cars, and now he was worried and wondering if he'd been caught.

Bolan did not have time to wait the guy out. He brought the Beretta up and closed the distance be-

172

tween them with a silent but shattering Parabellum cruncher.

Bolan fed that body in on top of the other one, closed the door, and went on to the house.

Except for the front gate, that should have taken care of the outside men.

Bolan did not give a damn about the front gate.

He went in through the French doors off the courtyard and turned into the east wing, passing through a darkened hallway and into the fully-lighted dining room.

A television eye glared at him from a wall station. He phutted a bullet through it and continued on past the butler's pantry and into another short hallway without changing pace. Over a door in the far wall was another eye. He moved swiftly beneath it and covered the lens with his hand, rapped on the door, and said, "Hey!"

A bored voice, mechanically reproduced through a speaker beside the television camera, responded with, "Yeah, what."

"You got some eyes out in there?"

"Well . . . yeah. I was just fixin' to call about it. What the hell is it?"

No false security, eh?

"Open the damn door and I'll fix it," Bolan growled. "What the hell you been doing, sleeping?"

"Hell no, I told you I was just . . . ."

A buzzer sounded and the door opened to Bolan's pressure.

He stepped inside and a fat man with a face like red wine cried, "Whuuup" and made a lunge toward his shoulder holster.

The Beretta won the race by a lifetime. Blood and pulpy flesh and splintered bone splattered across the

173

television monitors. Bolan stepped back to the hallway and clicked the door shut.

The next stop was the kitchen.

Only a night light was burning and no one was present there. He found the power panel and a thoughtfully-placed flashlight in a little alcove near the door and pulled the main disconnect, removed the cartridge fuses, and dropped them into a garbage can.

There were no lights—nor anything else electrical—operating in the big joint now.

Bolan was standing in total, choking darkness.

He stepped to the window and checked the progress of the sun, then he snapped on the flashlight and went quickly back through the dining room.

People were astir when he reached the entry hall at the front of the house. The sentry dog was growling uneasily and his handler was trying to calm the big animal. Several shadowy figures had stepped in through the doorway from the west wing, swearing and groping their way through the darkness.

Bolan was the man with the flashlight, and obviously the man with the answers.

A snarlingly unhappy face appeared in the spot and the guy asked, "What the hell happened?"

Behind that beam, Bolan knew that he was practically invisible. He replied, "Power failure. Just relax."

"Relax hell," another voice protested. "You can't see your hand in front of your face in here. How long's it gonna be out?"

The rest of your life, Bolan wanted to say. Instead, he said, "Sun's rising pretty soon. If you're scared of th' dark, go outside. It'll be light out there in a minute."

"Fuck that," somebody commented.

"Sounds good to me," someone else argued. "Where the hell's the door? Shine that light over on the door, huh?"

That ancient animal dwelling within man still found himself nervous and uncertain about the dark.

Bolan obligingly spotted the door with the flashlight.

He counted five men moving through the open doorway.

Then he told the man with the dog, "Take that bastard outside and shut 'im up . . ."

The guy did so, without a murmur, leaving the door open.

Bolan crossed over and into the west wing. It was set up with a hallway running the full length along the center, doors opening onto offices and rooms to either side.

One of those doors now stood open and people were loitering about in uneasy attitudes along the darkened hallway, and all eyes turned toward the beam of light from Bolan's flash.

Bodyguards, Bolan read it.

He announced in a loud voice, "Power failure. Don't worry, it'll be okay in a minute or two."

One of the men growled, "It's already been a minute or two."

Another door opened then, farther down, admitting a feeble seepage of yellow light into the hall. According to Grimaldi's diagram, that should be the conference room.

A large man moved through the open doorway, and a man close to Bolan hastened to explain to the new arrival, "Power failure, boss. It's being taken care of."

Another close voice demanded, "Hey you, guy, give the boss the flashlight."

The big man said, "Never mind, we got candles. Relax, it's not the end of the world. This is Haiti, not Baltimore. Things like this happen here. What's the matter? Can't you boys read your cards in the dark?"

Someone chuckled.

The big guy said, "It'll be daylight pretty soon. Relax." He spun gracefully around and went back through the doorway.

And then Bolan realized who he was.

Big Gus Riappi.

He called out, "Gus!"

The guy reappeared, looking edgy and disgruntled in the flickering yellow light, but the voice was smoothly controlled. "Yeah. Who is that?"

"Frankie. Tell Sir Edward a courier is here."

"A courier from what?"

"Hell I don't know. Came in by helicopter. He's in a hell of a sweat. Says we should tell Sir Edward he's here."

"Yeah, I thought I heard a chopper. Where is he?"

"Went upstairs, to the suite. Just before the lights went out."

"Okay, I'll tell him. We're almost through in here."

Riappi went back into the conference room. One of the bodyguards muttered, "It's about time they were through in there."

Another one said, "Shut up. They'll be through when they get through."

"I just meant, shit, since midnight f'chrissakes. How long does it take to shuffle a few heads around?"

"I said shut up."

So Bolan had another reading. As he had suspected, the Caribbean Carousel was being dismantled and put back together again—same game, same rules, different players. And it was being engineered from Port au Prince.

He kept the flashlight beam well in front of him and casually announced, "That courier must've just come from San Juan. He says they're having a party at Glass Bay."

The guy with the hard voice came to stiff attention and said, "What's that?"

"Glass Bay's celebrating. I guess they got reason to."

Bolan received a totally different reaction than the one he was expecting.

The guy spun around and walked stiffly to the door of the conference room, rapped lightly with his knuckles, and went in.

"That fuckin' Lavagni is the luckiest shit alive," someone muttered.

Bolan agreed, "Yeh, he's lucky."

Big Gus reappeared, the bodyguard in tow. Bolan thoughtfully put the spot on the floor at Riappi's feet. The big guy glared at the invisible entity behind the flashlight and growled, "What's this about Glass Bay?"

Bolan replied, "Hell, Gus, the guy just said they're having a wild celebration. That's all I know."

"Well I'll be a son of a bitch," Riappi said disgustedly. He pushed his chief bodyguard aside and returned to the conference room.

Bolan said, "What's he so steamed up about?"

"You'd be steamed up too if you'd just lost what he just lost," the talky one told him.

The other guy said, "Flukey, shut the hell up!"

177

"Well I just—"

"Get on back in the tank!"

"Well dammit, it's—"

"All of you! Back in the tank! Open the goddam drapes or something, shit—use your goddam heads for a change!"

Bolan watched as three hardmen filed into their watchroom—the "tank." The head man looked toward Bolan and growled, "What the hell're you waiting around for?"

Bolan waggled the flashlight and replied, "I'm waiting for Sir Edward."

The guy grunted and went into the conference room.

Bolan leaned against the wall and counted the seconds. Not many were left. Very soon now the sun would be sliding up out of the sea and the Executioner would be losing his invisibility.

Then that door down there opened, and a tall straight man emerged to stare coldly into Bolan's light shield.

And yes, this had to be the guy ... and he was no black man. He was also no white man such as Bolan had ever encountered in the usual Mafia circles.

He had that soft antiseptic scrubbed chairman-of-the-board look, that Wall Street image of solid respectability and impeccable social background, the kind of guy you wouldn't expect to yell *shit* if he were drowning in it.

Bolan had never seen this man before, but he'd seen dozens of duplicates gazing benignly from the pages of national magazines and from the financial pages of big city newspapers.

He was Mr. Plymouth Rock, WASP of the ages,

president of that corporation and director of this foundation and chairman of a dozen charity drives.

He was Mr. Good, protector of the nation's morals and preserver of a society's cultural treasures.

Or, at least, he must have been at one time.

And Bolan found himself filling with rage and shaking inside over this particularly revolting new look in "the criminal type."

In the name of what golden graven god did a guy like this put down every human trust and confidence and turn upon his society to cannibalize, loot, rape, and ruin the upward movements of his fellow man?

Yes, this was a big one. This guy didn't steal nickels and dimes. He built and perpetuated ghettoes, created junkies and filled the jails with habitual criminals, destroyed lives and disrupted families by the wholesale ... and all for the love of the lousy buck.

Yeah, and Bolan knew now why the fates had directed the Executioner into the sunny Caribbean ... he knew that he had come for just this man, this man alone, the biggee.

He choked back his anger as he said, "Sir Edward, a guy is dying to see you."

"Yes, so I'm told," the guy replied smoothly, and the voice fit the rest of him. "Lead the way, please."

"You'd better go first, sir," Bolan suggested. "I'll keep the light ahead of you."

"Very well."

The guy moved on along the hall, following the spot, and walked past the door to the "tank."

Bolan fell in at his side and the Beretta found soft flesh just below the ribs and the icy voice of the

Executioner recommended total silence and faultless behavior.

Sir Edward stiffened slightly but moved on without a falter to the end of the hall, across the reception room, and out through the French doors to the courtyard.

They headed across the grounds toward the north wall, and the eastern horizon was glowing reddishly when Mr. Clean decided to risk a confrontation with his captor.

He came to a halt and turned a haughty gaze upon the man behind him.

And then the eyes wobbled, and that board-chairman jaw dropped, and Sir Edward gasped, "My God! It's Mack Bolan!"

"That's who," Bolan replied coldly. "The bells toll for *thee*, Edward."

"Now just one moment! You have allowed yourself a hasty and dangerous conclusion!"

The guy was trying to dazzle him with his goodliness.

Bolan said, "And what's that?"

"I am not associated with the Mafia!"

The graveyard voice told him, "Of course not. The Mafia is a legend, it doesn't exist."

"Oh it exists, Mr. Bolan. Believe me it exists. But my God, man, surely you can't believe *I* could be mixed up in anything like that!"

Bolan's stomach rolled. He shoved the guy toward the wall. "Move," he commanded.

The image was falling apart before Bolan's eyes.

The face went mean, the gaze crafty, and the voice turned to pure oil. "All right, then, let's be realistic. You're a grown man, Bolan. What do you want? From life, what do you want? I'll get it for you. Your heart's desires, riches beyond imagination, power beyond measure. Women! The most beautiful and desirable women in the world, Bolan—a sultan's harem! Think of that! Think of—"

"Shut up," the voice of death commanded. "I've got what I want."

"My God, man, be reasonable!"

"I didn't come here to judge you, Edward. I came to execute you."

The dissolved image was pleading, "I can give you—" when the Parabellum punched through the bridge of the nose and expanded into the brain, and another evolutionary backslider seceded from the three-dimensional world.

The Executioner stood over the sorry remains, and he dropped a marksman's medal onto the still chest, and he said, "You can't give me a damn thing, Edward."

As he scaled the wall, Bolan could hear the sentry dog whining somewhere off to the front, and he could hear the comforting sound of a rotary wing churning up the atmosphere in the very near distance.

He threw a final look at "the mansion in the rocks" —and it looked much more impressive in the dark.

He grunted, "Hell, it was easy," dropped to the rocks outside, and hurried off for a meeting with a good honest wop.

EPILOGUE

"We're clear," Grimaldi announced as the forbidding mountains receded to their rear and the little chopper sped on into the rising sun.

They were the first words to be spoken since lift-off.

"You're worth your price, Jack. Don't sell yourself so cheap from now on."

The pilot chuckled and said, "I guess you're not going to tell me how it went, eh."

"It went," Bolan replied. "The big one is gone."

Grimaldi sighed and turned his attention to his instruments. A moment later he said, "There'll be another one before they can get him planted."

Bolan sighed also. "Well, I'm still around," he said.

Grimaldi laughed nervously. "Don't pay me any mind, Bolan. You're doing a hell of a job on the mob. You'd never know how good unless you were on the inside looking out."

"Thanks."

"You're welcome."

There seemed to be little more to be said.

Presently Bolan shifted about in his seat and requested, "Keep your eyes open for a Chris Craft deep sea cruiser, eh."

183

"You expecting one?" Grimaldi asked, sliding a sidewise gaze toward his passenger.

"I don't know. Just keep your eyes open."

"I can drop lower."

"No, this is okay."

"I, uh, I sort of had the idea that those numbers you sent down from Glass Bay were coordinates. Is it still a secret?"

Bolan smiled and told him, "A lady was worried. I had to promise her a final report."

Grimaldi rolled his eyes as he replied, "If it's the lady I'm thinking of, I'd promise her anything."

Bolan chuckled and said, "Especially with a gun in your throat, eh?"

Grimaldi laughed, "Yeh. You're really expecting a rendezvous, eh?"

"Just by radio. And ... she may have decided to hell with it."

"Maybe not. Look away at ten o'clock—about, uh, ten degrees from horizon."

Bolan lifted the binoculars and scanned the area suggested.

A grin creased his face and he said, "Put me on international distress."

"You're on."

Bolan pressed his throat-mike and said, "Hello Eve, this is Adam."

"Thank God," came the instant reply. "Are you well?"

"Perfectly. Uh, the kill is over."

"Not quite," she said. "You left a lingering casualty."

"Where?"

"Right here."

Grimaldi chuckled and Bolan sent him a stern

look. He told Evita, "Parallel paths have a way of crossing from time to time."

"Let's try," she suggested.

"Bet on it," he said. "Goodbye, Big Eve."

"Adios, Tall Adam."

Grimaldi made a pass directly over the boat, and it looked like a kid's toy on a placid pond. Bolan watched it out of sight, and then his eyes clashed with Grimaldi's.

The pilot winked understandingly and asked, "She come all the way up here just for that?"

Bolan sighed. "Some corners of hell you just can't hang onto, Jack, without a bit of reassurance here and there."

"Whatever that means," the pilot said soberly.

Bolan turned his gaze to the horizon.

How many men had he killed this week?

Enough.

Hell yes, enough for this week's work.

The ones he hadn't killed would be waiting for him somewhere, some time, maybe around the next corner of the map, maybe tomorrow, maybe even tonight.

He thought of Riappi, and the awful embarrassment the big guy would have to face. How would he explain it to his bosses?"

There was more than one way to kill a man, Bolan realized.

But, yeah, for this week of work, it was enough.

Next week, now ... well, next week would be a whole new story.

The world died 'twixt every heartbeat, and was born again with each new perception of the mind ... and death itself was no more than an unusual perception.

Sure. Next week would accommodate a large number of unusual perceptions.

Bolan settled back into his own little corner of hell, and went to sleep, and dreamed of paradise. For this time, the kill was over.

the EXECUTIONER by Don Pendleton

Relax...and enjoy more of America's #1 bestselling action/adventure series!
Over 25 million copies in print!

More bestselling action/adventure
from Pinnacle, America's #1 series publisher.
Over 16 million copies
of THE DESTROYER in print!

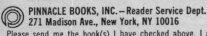

Best-Selling Sports Books
from Pinnacle